The Sifting Project

a novel

Mikaela Brewer

 FriesenPress

Suite 300 - 990 Fort St
Victoria, BC, V8V 3K2
Canada

www.friesenpress.com

ISBN
978-1-03-910994-0 (Hardcover)
978-1-03-910993-3 (Paperback)
978-1-03-910995-7 (eBook)

1. FICTION, LITERARY

Distributed to the trade by The Ingram Book Company

For Anthony,

who relentlessly believed in me when I couldn't believe in myself.

For my village,

you know who you are. I love you (more than coffee).

Table of Contents

CHAPTER 1

– We Choose –

Fall 1979, New Jersey

Penny frowned unempathetically at her hands. The lines on her palms weren't the same. They didn't match up at all. They curved around the meat of her palms and webbed frivolously up toward her thin, boney fingers. She tried to fold them like a book, the spine being an imaginary bridge between her pinkies and outer ridges of her hands. She brought them together, line for line, searching for a perfect reflection. They just didn't match. Of the many things she could be concerned about, her heart yearned for perfect hands while her prosthetic leg straps gripped her thigh like a leech and her loneliness ached to be noticed.

Is there a reason why this is important? Beck thought, leaning against a nearby light post, arms folded over his black t-shirt. It clicked on above his head and formed a large cone of soft yellow light over him. He subtly looked around. The street leading to the train station was lined in recently fallen golden leaves, which matched the line that separated traffic. It had made him think of the yellow brick road from *The Wizard of Oz* when he walked down it. Beck Brooks peered down at his watch: 5:36 p.m. It was just beginning to get dark. He might have been dressed a little too '50s for this trip. Tony had rushed him before he had time to think about all the ways he wouldn't fit into the fall of 1976, though, a significant portion of what they were doing didn't exactly fit into the 1970s. Beck's gaze skimmed the train tracks in front of him. There was a cool vapour rising off of them. The light post was positioned slightly behind the small sitting area, where Penny sat on one of the damp, rotting wooden benches. Through the mist that hung in the dense air, leftover from an early fall rain, smoke rose up over the trees and buildings. It might have been the first set of smoke columns, marking fall in the same shade of grey that undertones all black-and-white photographs. The train was coming soon, and Penny was going to get on. Beck still felt strange knowing her next moves, yet he watched her as if he didn't.

"She's dangerous for you, Brooks," Tony had said. "But the Sifters are cold to the world. The chances that they grow a soft spot for the people they sift through is pretty damn slim. My concern is that you are no Sifter."

Danger wasn't the word Beck thought of. He felt drawn to her, though not in the way he'd expected when he first saw her photograph. There was a sort of incoherent bracket around them, and brackets were what you always solved first. Exponents came second. Beck wondered why he was watching her panic about her hands, suspended in the air with the mist. She was observant and aware in a way that he couldn't comprehend. Everywhere he looked — the trees, the train tracks, the smoke, the houses, the crispness of colour against the sky, and Penny herself, were impeccably clear. It had to be impossible for Penny to be able to commit this much to memory, especially given that this was three years before present day. Beck pressed the blue knob on the side of the watch, bringing Tony's tracker to the small screen.

Penny, 28, October 10th, 1976, Princeton, NJ.

She looked about that age and it was definitely October. The trees around the station were every shade of orange, red, yellow, and brown, filled with air and life as they expanded into the sky like hot-air balloons. Their leaves fell in smooth leathery piles on the ground and blew up as the tracks rumbled with the approaching train, settling eerily slowly through the thick dampness of the air. Boots scuffed the drive as people hurried to the station in dark coats that repelled the cool humidity. Penny's coat was a warm burnt orange that stretched tightly across her broad shoulders. The colour clung to her body as if to rush away from what drew the leaves from the trees, and the pennies from people's pockets.

Penny's jet-black waves swished around her shoulders and arms with the breeze of frenzied bodies. Her sage-green eyes glanced up, and though they were like freshly annealed glass, the skin beneath them was dark enough to appear bruised and weathered from nights awake dancing with a maelstrom of thoughts. She turned her head over her shoulder, only enough to see him. She was deathly pale, almost luminous against the opaque black noise of the life around her. He held her gaze without realizing it, and felt their shoulders rising and falling in unison, mirroring one another's acceleration. Beck darted his eyes to his watch. *Shit.* How was he going to get on the train now? Penny was questioning if she had seen him before as she turned back to face the tracks. Beck slipped behind the trees, although this one's lack of leaves didn't help in hiding his face from anyone. *Another reason a jacket would have been smart, Tony.* Beck rolled his eyes, his back against the tree and the train blaring into the air. Once Penny looked back down at her hands, Beck darted behind the benches and onto the platform. As the train pulled in, he slipped in the door and sat down. He turned to make sure Penny got on at the other end. She didn't. Beck stood, panicked, and leapt off the train, hiding behind the post of the overhang of the station, white-knuckle gripping it as if *it* might board the wrong train with Penny still inside. He could feel his heartbeat in his palms. Penny hadn't looked up and was consumed in thought as the train pulled away. Wrong train, maybe? He was sure it was the right one. So, she was already deviating from her own memories. Was this what Tony had warned him about? Penny was now thinking about how her hair formed small ringlets in only a few places around her face, and how she had precisely one hundred freckles spotting her nose and high cheekbones, but yet her palms weren't perfectly lined. Her skin was almost a pale blue. She thought it completely impossible for skin to show longing, like the uncommonness of a blank sheet of paper in her apartment. She looked up at the sky, taking in the brightness of the pale grey as if it would help her catalyze the next moment. In a small leather satchel, she pulled a packet of folded parchment, wrapped carefully in purple-and-red cloth. She fished around for a pen, and once she found it, began to write. Somewhere, she thought, her parents must have made a mistake. Becker watched curiously and reverently as he always did when she did this. He wanted to ask her what these past few minutes had created in her mind, but he couldn't. She didn't know him yet. He had to progress in the right order. She didn't write for long, and now all he could see were her hands, folded limply open like a book in her grey-blue corduroys, as if she chose not to give them life.

Does she already know me here? Becker gripped the side of the wall tighter. She seemed oblivious to the events around her, but he knew she wasn't. Absentmindedly he watched her. What could he do? How was he supposed to sift through her memories if she could change them on the spot? Beck realized at this point, that he had to do more than simply observe her life. This was dangerous, and now he knew why as the stabbing pain of the cold air in his lungs reminded him that he couldn't save her. But here he was, crawling into the alleyways off of Penny Lane. It's easy to hate someone when your work revolves around living in their memories which can only be formed from their perspective.

"But not you, Pen," he whispered, almost silently. The stakes were vastly bigger than either of them understood. Beck had combed through two years of her memories from 1979 to 1977, and he needed to work quickly. He had nearly thirty more years to do. But the longing for these ten years when they were close in age ached in his bones. There was no after.

#

"Tony, I can't do this. Every time I go back she doesn't know me."

"Brooks, you have to trust me."

"No, you know, I don't. It's not better that way. Because I can't lose her. And the further I go back the more I realize how much of her life I've missed."

"But that's the thing. The more you go back the more you aren't missing it." Tony held up his scotch as if to toast. He always managed to give Beck little hints of his past when he drank, especially the parts he wouldn't speak of.

"Do you miss anyone?"

Tony paused, drawing in a long, crackling breath. "Yeah, Brooks, I did." His eyes glossed over but he never broke eye contact with Beck, peering almost coldly into his eyes. He wasn't going to say it, but Beck felt it.

"Well, I'm not going anywhere anytime soon," Beck said, meeting Tony's stare. Tony held it for a few seconds, and looked away, gulping down the last three swigs of his scotch. He wiped his face quickly, trying to hide the fact that he'd wiped his eyes with his sleeve along with his mouth.

"Beck?" Penny's assertive voice broke Beck from his own memory. He froze. It always struck him how confidently she spoke. He'd asked her about it once, and she had readily informed him of his biases. Right now he was afraid she could hear his heartbeat, but she still hadn't looked up.

On the south side of the city, and only the south side, could you find flaming-purple brush, wooden tracks perfectly aligned in smooth steel, and a train station with garbage that hadn't been emptied for weeks, it would seem. It couldn't be here, because this felt familiar. Beck had been here before. He looked at his watch again. This had to be wrong. It had to be wrong. The rule is you work backward, so that the person you're sifting never has a memory of you in their present. For Penny, this was 1976, at the moment. You sift through their memories from the present to the past. He wondered if he had made a mistake the last time?

Beck clicked through the memories in Penny's file until he found it and hesitated. He curved his view slightly, around the side of the train station wall again. Her head was tilted up at the sky but her eyes were closed. Her skin was glistening in the disappearing light, absorbing its coolness. He needed to talk to her. Sifters never built a connection to their project but she was different and this was different. Beck would never be a Sifter. He was afraid for her and now, slightly of her. He didn't want to leave her here as it got dark, unsure if she would be safe. No one was supposed to find her here — it wasn't one of her more vital memories. He clicked on the memory file in his watch, never taking his gaze off of her as the train station blurred like rain on a fresh painting.

#

She was supposed to be alone here. Somewhere north or south of Stokes Avenue, Madewell Brook was a sleepy corner of a village that wasn't made well at all. There was only an elderly rusted railroad dusted by obnoxiously red wildflower brush, lined by miles of golden dehydrated grass, overlooking an aggressive ocean on the left. Penny thought it ironic that the water was so close, just a few minutes climb down the cliff to the beach. The permanently bleached grass was forced to stare at the endless water, and never seemed to die as the water itself ripped and curled around stories of parties and knifed Bud Light cans, the occasional bottle of cheap wine and expired firewood. *Damn, poor grass,* Penny thought. She sat down and it crumbled like that turmeric powder her mom used to put in the crust of her chicken. She took off her prosthetic leg and glared at the green-and-white writhing ocean. "Fuck the ocean, eh?" she whispered, running her fingertips over the grass she hadn't crushed. It felt like straw, as if it could be swept into one of those expressionless scarecrows. "Ignorance can be bliss. You don't have a brain, so maybe you don't know that you're suffering. Don't go looking for one either." She tied a bright red-and-purple scarf around the middle of her thigh, right above where it disappeared. Beck had never asked about it and wondered if it meant anything. He supposed it was her mother's.

"Bet pennies won't even be a thing fifty years from now, like everything else the world neglects," she spoke to the scarf as she tied it angrily tight.

Beck fumbled to look at what the timer said: April 14th, 1979. His last registered sifting time was just before this, in December of '78. *She knows me here. I could go talk to her.*

"They will be to me," Beck answered her comment about pennies.

She looked up and smiled dully. "Oh, hi."

"You know this would be a great scene for a poem." He sat down beside her.

"Right," she half answered, never breaking her troubled gaze at the ocean.

"Pen?"

"Hmm? Yeah, it's pretty aggressively neglected, isn't it?"

"Well, I was thinking nice, but, okay." Beck laughed carefully.

"There's more beauty in the things we neglect than in the things we don't, I think."

"Why do you say that?"

"I'm not sure, but I tend to write about these things. Just need someone to read it."

Beck looked at her thoughtfully.

"What?" she asked.

"Nothing, you're just brilliant."

Penny smiled and stroked the scarf tenderly. Her hair was blowing wildly across her nose. "You need something from me?" She reached over to grab her prosthetic. He reached over top of her, blocking her arms, and tucked all the stray waves behind her ear.

"Not this time."

CHAPTER 2
– Whether Or Not To Listen –
September 1939, The Bronx, New York

Tony sat on the ground, his back up against the front wall of a red-brick house, facing the street. Had it not been red, it would have shown the liquid rust that poured from the eavestrough. His navy blue sweater was a wet ball of slush beside him, and he had untucked his white shirt from his black trousers. It suctioned to his body, so soaked that it almost looked like peeling skin. It was not a warm spring rain, but a harsh and icy rain that was degrees away from being the first snow in New York that year.

Tony had been splashed by five different cars on his long walk home and his only school sweater had taken the beating. Now, he sat outside, bathing in the cold. His parents didn't trust him and the evidence was in their favour. Thus, Tony didn't have a key and needed to wait until his father returned home from work to unlock the door. Tony's mother was an underpaid nurse and his father worked deep in the mines. He went to work at 2 a.m. and returned at 4 p.m. nearly every day. Scoliosis writhed in his back, his hands were achingly arthritic, and soot stuck to the oil on his body like insects to a spiderweb. They had little money and a quaint home to match, which they shared with another family who rented the upper half of the building. For homework, Tony often resorted to chalk on the walls in the corner of the house where his mattress lay upstairs. Paper was hard to come by, except in a few slightly less filthy bins at school. Tony preferred chalk though, which allowed him to expand his mind across the walls. Paper was too limiting. Despite his outstanding grades in school that no one cared to ask him about, Tony was a dirty thirties kid, and was reminded of it by his peers nearly every day. A war was to erupt in the coming years, and these were the people who could have told you it was coming because they felt it first. In reality, these were the people who were the most prepared for it and the least cynical. War was the epitome of their existence anyhow. Stories flooded the unspoken words in the walls. These are the intricate stories of life as it is — the stories which struggle to fend off the seasons but encase every detail in memory. These stories are plentiful, and most importantly, the ones which are heaviest to carry between generations. Bits crumble off as they are fumbled and dropped. Inside of themselves, people readily find and recite the stories that they've been taught, without questioning who is teaching them. There are many more stories inside besides these, simply resting, but without space to breathe. Together, if pumped with blood once again, they hold the power to challenge the ones that have been taught.

Even though his bones were saturated with rainwater like many others across the globe and just down the street, what Tony had against many leaders was a way of seeing life and refreshing the truth of what was unfolding around him. He had a small piece of paradise built within chaotic inevitable loss.

Tony stood and looked up at the second floor of the building. His thick dark hair poured a bucket of water down his back. He was looking to see if the window was open, which meant someone was home. The window was closed. Paul, his life companion, must still be at school.

Tony was so cold he picked up a stone and threw it at the top window of the house, cracking the glass in yet another place. He sat back down angrily and wrapped his arms around his legs, rocking back and forth. The water was squishing out from between his forearms and his knees, forming a little river down the sidewalk.

"Tony, what the hell!" a voice called down. Paul's voice was unmistakable — his accent was an odd mingling of New York and England, where his parents were born and raised. The window was so broken that Paul didn't have to open it to yell through.

Tony snapped his head up to see Paul's face in one of the holes in the window, squinting down at him as the rain came through. Even with little light in the sky, what was left of it always managed to hit and brighten his strawberry-blond hair.

"Why is your window closed?" Tony yelled up angrily. "I've been out here drowning for an hour! The brick isn't even red anymore!"

"Well that's just it, isn't it? It's raining. Why would I open the window?"

"Would you just come let me in?" Tony started ringing his sweater out. The water that poured from it looked like dishwater.

Tony could hardly hear Paul coming down the weathered box stairs to the front door. He had always been so lean. They both had, but Paul was the more gifted by far. The door swung open and Tony scuffled in, creating a thin river in his wake. Even though they both hated their small home and the epitome of their existence, it was just that — home. Because the families had become so close, they opted to share a larger kitchen and common space on the ground floor and arrange sleeping quarters upstairs. Tony ran straight to the fireplace and threw a stack of wood in. His father had taught him how to safely start the fire inside. Once he felt a warm blaze against his cold cheeks he called Paul to bring the kettle over. He could hear Paul searching for it in the small stack of pots and pans that they called their kitchen. Paul hurried over and put the kettle on the ring over the firepit. He had also brought two chipped mugs and the hot chocolate mix. Their mothers often reminded them that it was only for special occasions, but this was an exception, of course. Thankfully, the weather's unpredictability was a common exception living in New York. Tony and Paul both sat on the tattered red couch, stitched with patches of old quilts. The squares of the quilts had been sewn with clothing they'd outgrown, among other pieces of cloth that they could get their hands on — dishrags, burlap, scarves. Tony and Paul had both spent time wondering what story each piece could tell, and where that story was now. The fire breathed life into their tired, hollow faces. Their bodies came to a bright orange glow, simmering calmly to comfort the other. At 4:30 p.m. the light was beginning to evanesce from the windows, now permanently damaged by moisture. They huddled under the one blanket that Paul's mother had stitched, mesmerized by the way the light of the sun and the flame flickered through the foggy glass together. Their eyes grew droopy, and Tony would have fallen asleep had Paul not nudged him awake.

"You have to wait for the hot chocolate," he said smiling.

Tony nodded and sat up straighter, hugging his knees to his chest again. He had so little, yet he felt at peace waiting for his father to come home. He rarely saw his mother, except on Wednesdays when she didn't work. Paul's father, who also worked in the coal mines with Tony's, had been studying from old medical textbooks in his spare hours since he was a teenager. He had scraped his way through medical school bills by working in the mines and with some help from money left by his parents. Tony's father, Mr. Crypt, and Paul's father, Mr. Elliott, had been friends since high school when the Elliott family first moved to New York. Mr. Elliott searched for ways to finish his residency alongside working in the mines at night. Paul was certain his father would become a doctor, and that they would be able to move to some disparate place, far from where they were now. Tony's family, on the contrary, had always been somewhat lonely in New York, and Tony avoided thinking about the fact that Paul and his family might not be so close soon. With the war approaching, Tony prayed that it would be hard for Mr. Elliott to find a job, though he figured doctors would be sought after soon. He was utterly afraid for his mother and father who would likely be recruited for the war. Paul was afraid too, but he was positive his father's accolades in medical school would earn him a job in the city. He attempted to speak this into existence nearly every day, which Tony hated.

"We should really ask how to cook, you know," Tony said to break the silence. Their eyes still watched the fire.

"Why?"

"What if our parents go to war? They probably will, you know."

"Nah, my father won't. He's going to…"

"Get a job in the city, right," Tony finished. "It won't matter. They'll make everyone go. We're going to be here alone."

"So we can drink all the hot chocolate."

"Paul, I'm serious. We'd have no food!"

"We'll figure it out."

"No, I'll figure it out."

"Right, forgot you're the smart one. I'm just the sidekick, right?"

"I didn't say that."

"Well that's what you meant."

"No, I didn't. You're smart too, just not *as* smart," Tony laughed. Paul turned and punched Tony in the arm, and they began to wrestle and writhe around on the floor until they were out of breath, their stomachs ached from laughing and they heard a key jam haphazardly into the door lock. Tony kicked the hot chocolate tin under the couch and the boys sat back up on the couch. Their fathers entered through the front door, covered from head to toe in soot. Their faces were as readable as a children's picture book. They were noticeably exhausted, but they smiled big and their teeth looked as white as the snow was sure to be in a few weeks, against the dark hollowness of their faces and their thin, barely clothed, soaked bodies. The bowls below their cheekbones were as empty as their stomachs. Paul and Tony winced watching them peel off the thin coats they had, wringing them outside and hanging them up beside the door. Both boys loved their fathers, and to see them like this nearly brought them to tears. Eventually the two men closed the door behind them and came into the house.

"Good afternoon, boys," Paul's father said. Tony's father nodded behind him. He was trying, but there was a deep fatigue in his voice that was progressively more difficult to hide.

"Hi," Tony and Paul replied in unison, smiling and nodding.

"You make some hot chocolate?" Tony's father asked expectedly as he grabbed the dish soap from the kitchen area. There was no bathroom in the house, just a tub in the other corner of the one-room floor. There was also a shared outhouse in the backyard.

"We were about to," Tony replied nervously.

Tony's father motioned to the tin under the couch. "Why don't you make two extra cups before the mammas get home, huh?"

"I second that," Paul's father added. He began filling massive buckets of water from the pump at the sink and brought them over to the fire to warm up. Tony's father poured the dish soap into the tub and swirled it around.

"What are you up to?" he asked from across the room.

"Not much. We're still wet from the rain. Rather, Tony is because he sat outside waiting for someone to come home and open the door. He didn't know I was home already."

"Ah, sounds about right. Didn't think to knock?" Tony's father asked him, half laughing.

"No, I suppose not," Tony answered, more coldly than he intended to because he was embarrassed.

Paul and Tony's fathers made up their bath and wiped the dirt from their faces and bodies, while Paul and Tony sat pouring cups of hot water into the chocolate powder. Tony watched as the water bubbled up and the steam turned the powder creamy. He prayed for miraculous change like this, wondering if his own life could foam into an opulence that he could drink from a cup. Tony prayed in that moment. To whom he was praying he didn't know, but he prayed that his and Paul's parents would be sent to war. He made sure to ask that they would be spared, protected, and watched over. But he wanted them to go, all because he wanted Paul to stay. Tony felt he needed this moment forever. He didn't know who he was without Paul. A war evoked by mankind isn't necessarily tractable. Within the mastery of the web of plans, Tony needed Paul, and the world would soon need Tony. Tony's selfish prayers basked in a monolith of hesitant complies, but as most choices go, this one was not without an unfolding of lessons, foundations, repercussions, and necessity.

#

Tony sat up in his corner of the room upstairs while Paul slept. He sat on the edge of his mattress fiddling between the yellow and white chalk, trying to do his homework by moonlight. Although this made it more difficult, he thought it more of a challenge, and more peaceful. He only had enough paper to write out what was to be turned in at school, so he practised problems on the walls with chalk. Tonight he was unable to concentrate. He swivelled on the bed and stared out at the moon. A submarine of anger and fear gurgled the water underneath the equations intermittently. Tony was two grades ahead of his age, and thus, his only friend was Paul. Tony needed him more than he would admit out loud, even if he poked wittily at his every move. He turned and looked at Paul sleeping with an apparent peace of mind that Tony could never recognize inside of himself. A cruel idea bobbed like a buoy in the rough waters of his mind, though within swimming distance. The adults were downstairs drinking the cheapest ale they could find. They were laughing and enjoying one another's company. Tony crept to the top of the stairs to watch for a few seconds, admiring their ability to find tenderness and sentiment in the midst of the under-world and wrath that they lived through each day. He sighed and turned to the corner of the room where Paul's mother and father usually slept. He inched over to the battered bookshelf that stood behind their bed, holding all of their belongings. He was looking for something in particular as he ran his forefinger over the spines of the battered medical books, reading each one's name in his head. He stopped when his eyes fell on one he hardly recognized. Mr. Elliott rarely had this book in his hands, and it was the book which he had primarily studied from to get into medical school. Tony was sure Mr. Elliott would have hidden it here. He opened the book to a small divide in the pages, already created by something that didn't belong, resting patiently between the pages. Sure enough, there it was — Mr. Elliott's Rochester Medical School degree. He was one of the first to attend, not long after it opened in 1921. Tony silently closed the book and placed it back on the shelf, bringing the diploma with him. His intentions were above and beyond his moral capacity. He was acting purely out of emotive fear. Tony lay on his mattress and tucked the diploma under his pillow, softly closing his wet eyes.

Not long after Tony had begun to drift off, he was awoken by the adults climbing the stairs clumsily. The stairs creaked under their weight in an agonizing, groaning pain. One of these days they would fall through.

"Oh, how I wish they wouldn't grow up," Tony's mother slurred. One thing Tony knew now is that they all spoke markedly more truth when they drank.

"Tony better grow into that brain of his. They are both such smart young men," Tony's father commented.

"They aren't men just yet," Paul's mother added, kneeling down to kiss Paul on the forehead, and then Tony. "We should get going to the hospital." She motioned for Tony's mother to follow her. Tony and Paul hated the strain their nursing shifts brought, swelling their ankles and severing a piece of what was left of their young spirit each time. The floor moaned somberly as the women dragged their sore bodies between the two sleeping boys, simply to wish them goodnight.

"We should head out too," Paul's father whispered. "Sleep tight, boys, we love you equally as boys or teenagers." He laughed as he ruffled Tony and Paul's hair, knowing that they were awake. Tony felt a small tear form in his eye, but nothing was going to stop him now. He listened for the shuffling of them packing meagre bags and heading out the front door, into the night of morning, still a little drunk. As the door closed behind them, it sent a cool burst of breeze breathing up the stairs.

The morning was ever so slightly approaching in streaks, casting a thick blue through the windows of the house. It was equally eerie and refreshing. Once he was sure they had all left, Tony walked softly down the stairs to the fire with firm intent. The water-damaged glass of the windows was foggy, mocking, and contorting the bits of colour in the sky as they pushed through the pane. Tony sat cross-legged in front of the embers, and blew on them to ignite a paltry blaze. In almost a trance, he tore the degree into pieces and one at a time watched them nestle into the ruins of wood and burn to soot. He watched as his chance of loneliness was wisped away with the last shred of blackened paper. A jarring pain startled his chest, which he would feel for the rest of his life. He heard footsteps on the stairs and turned rapidly to see Paul walking down, rubbing sleep from his eyes.

"You okay? Why are you up?" he asked.

"Uh, I couldn't sleep," Tony replied sheepishly.

"What's on your mind?" He came down the stairs and sat next to Tony, bumping his shoulder against his own.

"I'm just thinking about the war, and how much I don't want our parents to go. I really want your father to get a good job as far away from it all as possible."

"No, you don't."

"What?"

"I know you want me to stay."

"Well I do and I don't. It's hard."

"I know."

The two boys sat in silence and watched the flames lap up over each other until the sun drowned the bright orange and yellow. They put the flames out with the leftover bathwater and went to school as usual. Paul sensed guilt in Tony. He was never this quiet, but Paul couldn't think of anything Tony could have done that would make him feel guilty. For the next year, they went about their usual days, until mid-September of 1940, when shame and regret began to perforate Tony's heart.

#

When the military officers knocked on the door, Mr. Elliott's medical degree couldn't have kept him home, though he tried to wield it as a shield against enlistment. At ages twelve and fourteen, Tony and Paul didn't know that their fathers were mandated to serve regardless. Later that evening, the four adults sat helplessly stunned, discussing what happened next. Both Tony and Paul's mothers were called up as field nurses. Tony and Paul listened to the uncomfortable silence from upstairs. Paul's uncharacteristic anger unfolded on Tony.

"Did you do something with it?" Paul asked through his gritted teeth.

Tony couldn't lie, but he couldn't tell the truth either. He didn't consider his silence to be an admission of his actions, but to Paul it was enough.

"How could you?" Paul sneered. "You're putting their lives on the line!"

"They will be fighting for and protecting our country, Paul."

"You didn't do it because you wanted to be patriotic, Tony. You did it because you're a selfish asshole."

"He's not even done residency! He's not a doctor yet! He'd be going to war anyway!"

"No, you're wrong. A medical school degree would keep him here. They need doctors here to look after soldiers when they bring them back. Now he'll be the soldier coming back. Maybe not coming back. You selfish fuck."

His rage and anger shocked Tony. Paul's face was the same colour as his hair and Tony didn't know what to say. He hadn't been thinking when he acted, and now he substantiated the magnitude of what he had done in his mind.

"You were going to leave me here alone."

"Did you really think we wouldn't bring you with us? Are you that shallow?"

Tony put his head in his hands. His tears left a grainy trail of salt on his cheeks. He looked up and made eye contact with Paul, whose face was wet and hot. The tension held as a rope harnessed to walls, as unforgivingly tethered as the written word of the constitution. Their friendship would become a partnership for survival. They had been content with being all each other had, but now they truly were when they least wanted to be.

For months afterward, they moped lifelessly throughout the house with chapped throats and cracked lips from not speaking, trying to fend off the seasons with a few bundles of cotton, the nickel savings they dug up in the backyard and what little money their parents left them. The house decayed exponentially, taking the colour with it, and appearing more like the sepia photographs tacked to the one wall not damaged by dampness. The roof collapsed over the firepit, making it nearly impossible to keep warm, as the winter air whipped away any heat. The saturated cold nearly killed Paul from pneumonia in February of 1940, seeping into his forgiving heart, as he pushed away Tony's pleas to help. Only when he became deathly ill, laying in Tony's arms as lifeless as the house stood, did he allow Tony's immense love and fear to nurse him back to health. Running snow through Paul's hair and over his patchy skin smashed the valves in Tony's heart. It froze and scarred his fingers, forcing him to remember and preserve the joy he felt by simply existing next to his best friend.

A year later, in February of 1941, they received word that a bomb had hit the tent where their mothers worked as nurses. They wept alone for days, their aching backs facing the other. All four of their parents had been writing to them, though they received few complete letters undamaged by the weather or censorship. Sharing what little they had left of their mother's words was all they spoke about. Two years later, in 1943, they were in their third year of high school. They had stretched their minds trying to cope with the war unfolding around and between them. Their grades had never been better. That October, they received MIA telegrams about their fathers, and a week later, confirmation that the bodies had been found.

With eyes as pale as the foggy fall, they scraped themselves from the house, along the sidewalk together, a few metres apart as if one of them could infect the other with the death that hovered around their eyes and hollow bodies. The bowls carved beneath their cheekbones and ribs were spooned clean, and they dragged open the door of the bakery begging for jobs. They both spent their nights gazing blankly and painfully at the white of the moon, which was companionless aside from the light of the stars, unreachable, and millions of years in the past.

#

Although Paul would never forgive him, he and Tony rekindled a piece of what their friendship had once breathed in their final year of high school and the final year of the war in 1945. Paul brought Susanna home, a girl with a head of warm red flames compared to the torrid heat of his own. Tony saw something in Susanna that might heal and bridge their delta of brokenness. What Tony didn't expect was to drown in her spirit, aptitude, and inclination toward academia that the three of them found solidarity in. Tony occasionally wondered if he felt such a connection to Susanna because she was a rendition of Paul, like a prologue to the same book of poetry. But she stood strong alone. She never let him speak for her, though she let him lift her voice and her thoughts. She was brilliant in observation, noticing trends that escaped both Tony and Paul's fatigued, century-old gaze.

Frequently, Tony found himself watching the two of them, unwilling to admit how reverently he loved these two people. He also knew that their feelings were not congruent. Paul knew, through the overcast attic of his mind, that he'd do anything for Tony. Neither of them would speak of their affection for one another, or their innate sense of compassion for the other until the dusk of their lives. Temporarily, Susanna's brief influence would spark the dusty lamps between them, just enough to brighten the room, and enable them to see one another for the next few decades.

Tony and Paul sat beside each other in silence, backs against the concrete walls outside the public library, waiting for Susanna to gather a few extra books. Even this was a step forward.

"Paul, I..." Tony started.

"Don't push your luck." Paul stood and walked into the library. He listened for Susanna's boots against the tile, and found her reading Richard Feynman.

"Left Tony out there again?" she asked, her eyes still scanning the pages.

"I'd rather talk to you." Paul leaned against the shelves, crossing his arms.

Susanna smiled. "You can't go on like this, you know. I see the way you two look at each other. You need each other."

"How do you know?"

"I know a lonely strive for power when I see it."

"I don't follow."

"Right now, science is powerful. It's this big thing out in front of us. But it has multidirectional potential. We have to consider whose hands it's in."

Paul's brow furrowed. "But you're doing it."

"I'm doing it because I love it for the stories I see in it. I don't want the power men have with science. I don't want to be awarded the other side of the same quarter. I love science because I see a power in it on the pennies in people's otherwise empty pockets. That power is between you and Tony too."

"How?" Paul was irritated by her maturity, and unconvinced.

"What do you think allowed you to live all those years in the house alone? Science?"

"No, but..."

"You understand each other's suffering." Susanna pulled one last book off of the shelf and wrapped her arms around the bundle. The light above her head flickered. "That's the cue!" She smiled, grabbed Paul's hand, and tugged him down the aisle.

#

Susanna was incandescent. She aged with Paul, both a few years older than Tony, and grew up in an upper-middle class family in upstate New

York, but she was a minimalist outside of her work. When Paul and Tony received partial scholarships to attend university for astrophysics in the spring of 1945, Susanna's parents kindly paid the remainder of their way. Susanna had been fascinated by their studies, but she was drawn to the beauty of neuroscience. In college, intimacy between the three of them planted roots like the bristlecone pines in California. Tony and Paul reventured into conversation when Susanna wasn't there, and temporarily, Paul forgot about the life they had lived before then. Even so, Susanna was no cure for tension, nor was she immune to intensifying it. Her vibrancy infiltrated much more than her intellect.

After a Saturday night party in early 1946, Paul left early to finish apparently impending physics problem sets in the library, leaving Tony and Susanna to wander down the cold cobblestones, creating a new pathway to their three-bedroom apartment. But as the ethanol suspended in the frozen air, leaving cookie crumbs of passion and truth, something deeper was milked from reverence. Thinking it harmless but nevertheless vowing never to tell Paul, Susanna never thought her carelessness that night to be relevant until she was hovered over the toilet puking. In the clinic an hour later, a familiar tale was told to the usual unsuspecting, though not naive victim.

At noon, Susanna waited outside Tony's chemistry class and gripped his arm, pulling him aside.

"Susy, what the hell?" He could see the agony in her face, lined like the stories of a riverbed. She held his hands in hers and looked up into his eyes, which melted him.

"Tony, I'm pregnant."

"What?" Tony asked, shivering.

"I'm pregnant," she whispered through gritted teeth. The small, sharp noise found its way through to Tony's hands and fingernails.

"I heard you, but you're telling *me*, which means?"

"Yes, I think it's you."

"God." Tony pulled his hands from hers and put them on his head. He wasn't nineteen yet.

"We can't tell him. I slept with him not long after you."

"Well then how do you know it's me?"

"I don't, but I can feel it." Susanna looked down at the checkered floor. The two colours were hardly dissimilar, but she could clearly see where they diverged.

"That's not good enough." Tony felt the feverish heat in his cheeks. He didn't wonder how she could know it was him. Susanna was unfalteringly like this — brilliantly observant.

"Well we'll cross that bridge when we get there. I've got to go."

"Susanna, can we talk about this? I don't understand."

"Don't understand what? Tony, we're in a public place right now and I have class."

"And class takes precedence over this? *You* came here to tell *me*."

"Yes, it does."

"Interesting. You don't have any feelings at all, do you?"

"For you? Yes, of course I do. I just," she paused, looking down at the snow on her boots. She kicked them together to clear it off. "I love Paul, you know that."

"Yeah, I suppose I do," he paused, his voice cracking. "Do you ever wonder how I feel?"

"Tony, I'm sorry."

"Thought so."

Susanna looked at Tony sympathetically. Her heart groaned. She loved Tony too, but she didn't know how to tell him no, without losing him. She also knew how Tony felt, about both her and Paul. Tony's double heartbreak tossed like tumbleweed in the sands of her mind.

"Tony, we both love you." She smiled weakly and hurried away down the hall, feeling his pain following her beyond its reach. Tony watched her leave, though he couldn't be angry. He had too much to lose. If Paul did find out, Tony worried that the haphazard stitches holding them together would rupture for good this time. His heart thudded under the weight of two unforgivable things in the span of six years.

#

In the years that followed, Susanna raised a daughter with the often desultory help of Paul and Tony, which Susanna tried desperately to be thankful for. The three of them had grown in anxiety and suspicion since the child fell into their hands. Susanna felt for Paul, as her daughter grew to look much like her father, sprouting effervescently into his mannerisms with little prompting. Susanna loved the name Penelope, Penny within it, and especially the root — Pen, after Elizabeth Barrett Browning's first son. Susanna hated her own name, and felt it to be monosemy. Penny's was a lyrical translation between rigidity and fluidity of observation, holding authenticity in each — a pen, a penny, and a Penelope — the three sides of the Pythagorean triangle. Susanna longed for a symbiotic relationship between her research and her thought. She longed to be able to create and weave it herself.

#

In the fall of 1949, Tony and Paul were interning with the United States government in the early stages of the development of NASA in Washington, D.C., where they now lived with Penny and Susanna, who hadn't worked since Penny was born. Other ideas stirred in Tony and Paul's thoughts, motivated by the fear of loss, rather than curiosity in the ability to clean the roots with meaning.

On a cold, hostile Friday night, they sat on the feeble couches of their apartment, the wires gracing the ceiling and walls like string lights. They drank cheap wine and avoided required research reading, thinking about the potential answers to questions that were never asked in meetings, or anywhere else for that matter. They were a little tipsy, but Tony's mind cleared, disentangling the jumbled network of thoughts into something legible. Susanna and Paul waited impatiently for the beginning and end of Tony's provocative verbal diarrhea, as they laughed, bantered, and enjoyed each other's company in the few spare moments they had. Tony ground his teeth as he watched Paul kiss Susanna. He didn't think he was jealous. He wanted to be happy for them, truly, but he felt something for them that confused him, and that was unparalleled in his teenage antics. He was drawn to them, and in a beautiful, mocking way they were drawn to each other.

Tony began thinking about how much wrong he had done Paul. He had thought, albeit briefly, about a way to mend what had been done. His mind tripped over the memory that Paul didn't remember being sick back in their old house. He wasn't sure if he was thankful or broken by this. Tony's heart had opened to his best friend, and Paul walked through the door, contrary to prevailing assumptions of hatred. Tony hardly recognized his own selfishness now. And so, the alcohol spoke for him as his mind oscillated between the past and present, settling on the thought that he couldn't bear to lose either of them.

"Hey, what if we could bring them back? Or go back in time to see them? What if we could?" Tony's words were slightly slurred.

"What are you talking about?" Paul asked, although he knew exactly who Tony was referencing.

"Our parents."

"Tony, leave that alone. It's in the past."

"I know it's not in the past for you."

"Don't pick at an old wound."

"You think I don't have a scar too?"

Susanna sat on the couch speechless and confused. She was the least drunk of the three, and admired the alcohol for finally surfacing this conversation between them. Tony kept rambling existentially.

"You ever think about souls? What are they? Where do they come from? Where do they go after death?"

"Tony, what?" Paul was confused now. Tony was on an irrefutable tangent and there was nothing either of Paul or Susanna could do about it.

"What if we could find where their souls went? What if we could find out where all souls go?" Tony climbed up and stood on the kitchen table, his scotch in hand, the open bottle splashing more brown splotches, soaking into the walls. His arms were swinging frantically to enunciate what he was trying to say. Susanna watched his hand pass within inches of the single light fixture in the room.

"Tony, would you get down, please?" Paul tried to ask calmly. Tony caught the irritation in his voice.

"Let's do it. Let's find out. We could be the smartest trio they've ever had. Paul, you and I practically emasculate them every day! All we have to do is test some things without them knowing!"

Susanna rolled her eyes at Tony's remarks.

"Right, without the defence department of the United States knowing. Makes sense," Paul stated sarcastically. He was angry now.

"Oh just give it a shot." Tony sat down on the table, his tormented eyes meeting Susanna's sympathetic gaze. He toppled onto his side, and almost off the table. Paul hurried over and cradled Tony's head before his neck snapped off the edge, his whiskey bottle smashing to the floor. Paul looked hard at his best friend, whose eyes smiled weakly up at him. He moved his dark hair out of his eyes. Paul sighed and motioned to Susanna to help carry Tony to bed. Susanna admired the two of them, unsure how they continued to stand by one another through years of lacerated hope. She couldn't help but wonder if it wasn't their doing, or even hers. She hugged Penny to her chest, stroking her dark hair, then set her down on the couch to help Paul.

#

Despite their arguing, in 1950, they began crafting something, though they weren't sure what yet. Tony and Paul were motivated by a melting pot of grief, anger, and love, which they found relief from when they worked together. Tony longed to undo his past. Paul longed to do whatever calmed Tony's incoherent agitation. Susanna only thought about the world she'd leave behind for Penny. Tony and Paul sought to find remnants of a soul in the atmosphere, using physics. Susanna searched for ways to theorize what that soul might be made of. She was limited by the resources of her time and space, though not by her mind. As usual, she was a few steps ahead of Tony and Paul, and often smiled to herself knowing that her research logically came before the findings of theirs. Nonetheless, the three of them worked simultaneously.

Piece by piece, Tony and Paul smuggled the little equipment that Susanna would need from the office to their apartment. As interns with a cruddy office to begin with, they built a small, secluded lab in the janitor's closet, down a few doors from their lab in the city. Susanna, perhaps, was the most intrigued, though she felt the heat and stench of danger for her and Penny, as it hung above her head brighter than the single bulb in their apartment.

Neuroscience history books from Greece, Rome, Egypt, Persia, Germany, and Russia lay open around architectural drawing paper, as Susanna mapped what might be relevant. She scraped together newspapers and magazines about the Institute of Higher Nervous Activity, which had just opened in Moscow, Russia. If something of a soul existed, she was determined to find it in the brain. Susanna had always believed that there was some compact construction of who someone was, somewhere inside the mind.

Penny spent hours on her mother's lap as electrical impulses, neurons, and pieces of the brain were mapped out, intricately connected on sheets of paper the size of her body. Susanna thought of Penny while she worked, often wondering what types of things she'd remember and which ones she'd forget when she grew older. She knew of infantile amnesia — in adulthood, Penny would forget and be unable to access her episodic memories before age four. Susanna drew frantically overtop of textbook cerebral angiographs. *If you no longer need your earliest memories, what if they are detached from their ability to reach your consciousness, and reconnected to build a space for something else?* Susanna began writing a theory of memory compartmentalization, and the potential for past soul storage — other souls, not one's own. Her hand glided across the page like skates on a freshly watered ice rink. She wrote of deeper connections with vivid memory in sleep, and the potential for finding more here. *Do our dreams hold synaptic connections to our own, and other's souls within us? Are souls made of memories?*

Susanna was passionate, but she was cautiously curious. She knew Tony's mind. She shared only what he and Paul needed — simple diagrams, and none of the detailed ones of the hippocampus, the brain's memory centre, with which she constructed her theory. As she worked, she was curious enough to find an answer, but also curious enough about danger not to share it.

In December of 1950, she moved to Salem, Massachusetts, with Penny. At the time, she and Paul had been engaged. Paul thought he was torn between the fulfillment of his job and the purpose he felt being at home with Susanna and his young daughter. He was actually torn between proximity to Tony and Susanna. Eventually, Paul thought it unsafe to make the commute to Salem on weekends to visit. He had made a decision she expected him to make since that day in the library, choosing Tony over her, though he wouldn't call it that. Susanna was content refining her theory with Penny, at a safe distance. Tony, in contrast, was insistent on seeing Susanna and Penny against Susanna's better judgement. Tony naively thought he could have everything, selfishly jumping at a semblance of chance when Paul informed him that he and Susanna had somewhat broken off. Tony refused to live afraid again.

#

"Not even a beer?"

"When we're done with this."

"Done with what, exactly? We're science brothers so that *this* is going to be in our brains for decades."

"That's my point," Paul stated.

"You know what's left of the accent only makes you sound smart."

"Right and how does the Bronx make *you* sound?"

"Well even Bronx sounds intelligent when you say it. Maybe if I went by Anthony. Mid-forties, accomplished, would need some glasses and a white lab coat instead of dirty blue."

"Right." Paul was concentrating on his work, but Tony liked prying for the frostbitten sarcasm. Paul was writing down celestial positioning from the telescope observations they had done early that morning in the wet brush clearing out back. It hadn't been combed or cleared in decades. In their late twenties, both were forced to love their work, mostly because they loved each other's distracting company. Paul had always been the more stable and consistent of the two. Tony was erratic and abstract but passionate and impulsively driven. His high motor and energy existed purely in his mind, hence why he had never been any good at sports. He lived for the fresh thinking his field required of him, captivated by the promise of discovery, though his immature charisma dampened his ability to tell infatuation from reverence.

For a branch of NASA's early origins, Tony and Paul worked in their handmade lab tacked onto Washington's government offices, toying a line of trust and fear. Down the hall was the janitor's office. Johannes went by Jan, and he worked around their required office hours to ensure that Tony and Paul's curiosity wasn't caught. Jan never understood why he had gravitated toward these two kids. Perhaps it was written in the stars they loved so much — an elliptical, ever changing attraction to conspiration. Or, he agreed with them — people tamper with what they know. People with power tamper with it beyond repair. Jan hoped that they would never lose that sight. It was one most people lost long ago.

"Besides, what could two interns know about this anyway?" he had mumbled to himself a year or so ago, when they first started their side project. He envied their keenness for the decades he'd made nothing of this space.

#

Susanna frantically packed a few folded diagrams and a thick red notebook in a leather folder, and buried it deep beneath the roses in her backyard.

CHAPTER 3

– Engage –

December 1953, Salem, Massachusetts

Penny skipped down the wooden staircase of an 18th century home that belonged to her great-grandparents. Later, she would hardly remember it, but today she hummed a Christmas tune she had made up in her head that morning. It was a fragmentary mix of "O Christmas Tree" and "Jolly Old Saint Nicholas." She ran her small fingers down the polished wood banister, and made a small downbeat with her voice every time her fingers hit a loop of silver-kissed green garland wrapped around the glossy wood. She leapt her two fingers over the loop, and tapped the spot in between loops with her nails, as if her fingers were reindeer hooves prancing over mounds of iridescent North Pole snow. She liked the sound of the tap that her fingers made. Her red dress swayed and shimmered in tune with her long black waves of hair, collected into a white ribbon. Her dancing caught the morning sun rushing in the front door of the house. Her green eyes sparkled magnetically, and though eyes are supposed to be the one thing that doesn't change from birth, Penelope's only became more green, like oxidizing copper. They held the monolith of joy she would carve and lock away. Draped over her shoulders was a small quilt that her mother had helped her make. Each patch was a square piece of something she'd worn — dresses, bonnets, coats, and her favourite: play clothes.

She didn't like her dress too much today. She liked to wear yellow because she thought it made her look like a bumblebee. Bumblebees were fuzzy and cute, but ladybugs were odd and too punctual. Penny was looking for her mother at the moment, but her mind kept wandering to each corner of curiosity in the house. Her eyes followed the flickers of light from the window, hoping she might catch a glimpse of her mother's hair at the end of a beam. Susanna's hair was a series of curved copper wire, untouched by the harshness of the world. It attracted sunlight like two lonely magnets, bronzing and brightening with each season, but remained a consistent place to snuggle into, like wildflower brush. Penny envied it deeply. She thought her mother was the purest person to walk the Earth.

Penny reached the bottom of the stairs and looked either direction. She took a deep inhale. She was searching for cinnamon in the air, though could only smell pine and ginger. Susanna always smelled like cinnamon and her nose was powdered with it. Every time she took a sip of her cinnamon-dusted coffee, it sprayed across her nose like tiny freckles. Penny's acute sense of smell usually enabled her to find her mother easily. Penny could smell other things too, many of which she stored as explicit memories. The first time she encountered a new scent, her other sensory input in that moment seemed to be packaged perfectly into a vivid film of the experience. Penny looked to her left toward the living room, which was filled with Persian rugs, wooden furniture, and a Christmas tree that reached all the way to the top of the twelve-foot ceiling. Penny waited for the day where she was big enough to climb the ladder and put the angel on top. Susanna loved red and purple tones, and thus the whole house was decorated in these colours. The rugs and paintings on the walls in the living room were electric at night when the candles on the tree were lit. Penny looked to her right, into the undersized kitchen considering the size of the house. It hadn't always been that small, but half of it had been converted to Susanna's office and workspace. Even the kitchen had been decorated in red-and-purple accents, with a large stained glass window projecting a sort of kaleidoscope over the sink. The light spraying through it made an enchanting watery pattern on the floor or wall of the front foyer depending on the time of day, close to where Penny stood. Penny listened for her mother's tinkering in her office but heard nothing. Maybe she had gone to the store? A few years prior, when Susanna had brought Penny here, the house had been left alone for decades. Convinced she would catalyze Penny's mind with a sanctuary of light and carefully crafted memory, she laboured over the house for weeks. Penny hadn't left the house since, and Susanna did her best to begin teaching her. Susanna feared the day she'd need to explain why she knew the things she did. Until then, she'd shield her.

"Mommy!" Penny called, as she wandered into the living room and sat cross-legged beneath the tree. Looking up at it hurt her neck. She laced her fingers behind her back and stared at the few presents. Penny never wanted much, though the waiting excited her. She noticed a shadow move behind the red curtains of the window beside the tree. She stood and wiggled her small body behind the tree and pulled back the thick curtain. Susanna jumped out and scooped her up into a warm hug.

"Mommy, you're squishing me!"

"That was my plan!"

Penny freed her arms and wrapped them around her mother's neck, cushioned by the volume of her hair and burrowing her little face into it. It smelled of spices and baking, of course most notably, cinnamon.

"You smell like Christmas," Penny giggled.

"Well it is Christmas Eve, isn't it?" Susanna laughed, placed Penny back down, and knelt beside her. Susanna's hair tumbled over her shoulders, tied away from her face in a red scarf which she had partially dyed purple. "You can open one of your presents, if you'd like?" She smiled into the lines by her eyes, which Penny liked to trace with her fingers.

"Really?" Penny answered excitedly, her eyes wide. She spun around and bent to pick one up from under the tree, but Susanna gently tugged her arm.

"I was actually thinking of the one behind the front door."

Penny frowned, confused, asking her mother with her eyes if she could open the door herself.

"Yes, go ahead."

Penny walked over to the door, reaching up on her tiptoes and using all her strength to pull the handle down. Susanna stood and grabbed the door itself above Penny's head and helped her. Penny peeked outside on the doorstep. A man was kneeling down with his arms open, snow sprinkled in his dark hair. The whiteness of the snow everywhere made his eyes look brighter. Penny grinned and leapt into his arms.

"Mr. Anthony!" she cried. Tony wrapped his arms around her and squeezed her tight.

"Hello, my perfect Penny! How many times have I told you to call me Tony?"

Penny pulled back against his arms. "And how many times have I told *you* that Anthony sounds better because you're a doctor?"

"Well, I suppose you're right." He pulled her back in for another hug, glancing up and winking at Susanna holding the door open. She rolled her eyes at him. They held each other's gaze for a moment before Susanna looked down. Tony glanced between the two girls, unsure who he adored more.

"Did you drive all this way to come see me?" Penny asked. Susanna had explained to her that Salem was far from Washington, where Tony worked.

"Absolutely, I'd drive anywhere to come see you!"

"What about me?" Susanna chimed in.

"That's a little more debatable." Tony stood, sliding Penny onto his hip and leaning in to kiss Susanna on the cheek.

"Is Paul coming?"

"Uh, no, he's with family."

"And you?"

"You're my family, right, Pen?"

"Yes! Mommy, can Mr. Anthony be my dad?" Tony and Susanna looked at each other, slightly startled. Susanna's sternness prompted Tony to try to lighten the mood. She had reluctantly agreed that Tony visit them. Tony and Susanna needed one another. The stories in their souls were intertwined at a magnitude which they didn't understand. Many are. To tell a story, one need only bridge the gap between the past and the present.

"What a wonderful idea! Can I be?" Tony asked Susanna, sticking out his lower lip.

"I'll think about it," Susanna said, catching a genuine curiosity in Tony's voice. She crossed her arms, peering firmly at the two of them, now heavily dusted in soft white.

"I need to make a quick trip to the store and get some things. Tony can you watch her for a while, please?" There was a slight note of fear in her voice that worried Tony.

"Why don't we all go? It will be a little Christmas Eve adventure!" Tony chimed.

"Yeah!" Penny agreed.

Susanna sighed, "All right, let's go." She smiled lethargically. Tony had caught the fatigue hovering around her. He reached around the corner inside the house and grabbed Penny's coat off of the hook beside the door, and swung her around onto his back. He set Penny down and she skipped toward the car. Tony grabbed Susanna's arm before she walked past him.

"What's wrong?"

"We need to leave. I'm getting some supplies and we're going to head south," she whispered, trying to push through Tony's grip, but he held her.

"Why?" Tony was confused and alarmed by her worry. She was always a bit worried, but this was different.

"It's because of a few things."

"Let me come. I'm not going to let anything happen to you."

"Well if that were the case you might not have come." She pulled free of his grip and headed toward the car.

#

They had been driving for an hour, sipping their coffee, and listening absentmindedly to the radio. Penny had fallen asleep in the back. Both Tony and Susanna could feel the tension in the silence between them.

"How are you both doing?" Tony tried asking kindly. He did want to talk to her.

"We're fine. Penny's different."

"How so?"

"Well she likes to be outside, for one. But she scribbles little stories everywhere. She's curious, but she won't be a scientist."

Tony sensed disappointment, which he didn't quite understand. "Does she have to be?"

"No, I suppose not. I just want her to observe the world for what it is, and for someone to believe her take on it, you know? I don't want her to be in the same situation I am, doing what I want but not getting paid."

"I think they're the same thing."

"What are?"

"Scientists, poets, writers — they are all observing these tiny details and then telling a story about it."

"Well sure, but one is taken much more seriously than the other."

"Unfortunately, yeah. But which do we need more? That's debatable. Pretty sure you said that at some point."

Susanna smiled. "Penny's mind is just so porous. She finds wonder in everything. The perfect prerequisite of a scientist."

"Or a poet."

"Do you always have to play devil's advocate?"

"Do you always have to so blindly believe in science?"

"Excuse me?"

"Science is amazing, Susy. But it's so easily tampered with. Not everything that people discover is good nor does it have good intention."

"We're not like those people, Tony."

"I'd agree but that's not my point."

"What is your point then?"

"I'm saying it's all just a depiction of observation. Penny can choose how she does that. One's not better than the other. They're both needed. The world needs a mind like hers. She listens. She's curious, like you said."

Susanna paused, shrugging her shoulders and letting out a long sigh. "I know. You're right. I just don't want someone to silence her because she can't speak in physics."

"What did you say were walking proof that poetry and physics are the same thing?"

Susanna sighed. "People."

"Right. Penny's just going to have to give them a reason to listen then. Don't lose faith in her before she even tries."

Susanna smiled weakly, gripping the steering wheel. "I have faith in her."

#

Browned snow flew up in the air, intermittently illuminated by harsh flashes of red and yellow. There was so much white that the ground and the sky were indifferentiable. The car flipped and pitched over and over in the air. Penny covered her eyes and screamed as the front of the car smashed headfirst into the ground and tipped over upside down. Glass fractured and splintered into bifurcated webs, spewing across the pavement, almost gracefully and purposefully, boasting that a single life is not sufficient in pursuit of what comes afterward. Penny squinted but her vision remained blurry. She tried turning her head to look around, only picking up brief images, flashing between darkness like the shutter of a camera. She sniffled, breathing in the scent of warm iron flesh and blood from her own nose.

#

"Pen, Penny!" Tony screamed, desperately trying to pull her free. He hadn't been injured, but Penny was falling in and out of unconsciousness, her eyes still taking photographs. She felt a sudden sharp pain sear through the bones in her right leg, just below her knee. She began to cry muffled tears before she was fully awake. She was unaware of how much time had passed, and as she tried to look around her, everything was dark and blurry from the pain and cloudy disorientation. She finally realized she was still in the car, and felt two hands wrap around her waist and pull her free. She also felt something crunch and tear off beneath her knee. She shrieked as the smooth whiteness of the road swirled into a chunky red and brown.

With horrified tears flowing from his eyes, Tony placed her upper half in his lap and unsteadily tied something tightly under her right knee. Penny screamed and writhed.

"Try to hold still, baby, please," Tony pleaded. She was losing a lot of blood, and he needed to tie a tourniquet, praying someone would stop on the road. Once he had, he wrapped his arms around her small shaking body, his hands sticky with red oil. "Shh, it's okay, it's okay, you're going to be okay, you have to be okay, stay awake, baby," he whispered. He could feel her breathing slowing. He was afraid she was dying instead of calming down.

Penny looked down at her leg. Below her knee there was nothing, and she saw red-and-purple cloth wrapped tightly around the stump, soaking in blood. "Where's Mommy?" Penny whispered, her voice quivering through her tears of terror.

Tony froze. He didn't want to look. His eyes glanced over to the car's driver's seat smashed unrecognizably into the ground. A dark, crimson red lake pooled around the headlights, littered with glass, remnants of a small bomb and locks of copper hair. Penny turned her head to follow his gaze and Tony turned it back. She had seen. They both lay still and wept. Tony held Penny tighter than he had ever held anyone in his life. "Penny, I love you," he whimpered, "don't leave me."

Penny couldn't speak, but she nestled her little body into his, his warm tears falling onto her face and mixing with her own. "I'm going to stay awake forever," she whispered weakly. Tony's body heaved around hers, rocking back and forth. He gritted his teeth so hard his gums bled.

As what was left of the shreds of her leg dripped into the ground, Tony's tears paced congruently. Susanna's blood flowed toward them, seeping under Tony's knees. All pieces of the earth hold bits of energy, which continue on an unapologetic path to become something else. As life is breathed out of one it is breathed into another. The fundamental pieces of what once lived do not pass away into absence. They flow vicariously to their next place, carrying pieces of each of their lengthy pasts.

CHAPTER 4

– Devote –

December 1953, Salem, Massachusetts

Penny sat in the hospital bed, her eyes blank and cold as she stared straight out in front of her. A thick set of casts, among many other coloured tubes and wires were attached to her body in uncomfortable places. She had realized her leg was gone only a few minutes ago, but it didn't numb her as much as the loneliness that created a bifurcating ache through the bones she had left. Penny was unaware that Tony had gone with her to the hospital. He had watched apprehensively as Penny's movements and tears drowned in the blood draining from her body. He watched the paramedics panic trying to keep her awake. Now, he was in the other room, receiving treatment for minor wounds which he angrily swatted away. They hadn't told him anything about Penny.

A doctor came in and sat down on the bed beside Penny. He had a kind, but tired face, and salt and pepper hair.

"Who are you?" she turned and asked, though her words hardly found their way around each of the tubes in her nose and mouth. She had lost a lot of blood and a lot of fluid.

"Hi, Penny, I'm Dr. Martin, and I am just here to check in on you. I need to talk to you about a few things."

"Okay," Penny sighed, glancing down at her leg.

"Penny, I'm so sorry, but your mother didn't survive the crash."

"I know."

"Oh?"

"I saw." Penny's bitter gaze was directly ahead, as blank as the dull grey stone wall that stared back. Dr. Martin looked at her concerned.

"Penny, how are you feeling?"

"I want to sleep," she lied.

"You go ahead and sleep, that is a wonderful idea. Your friend Tony is in the other room, and he will be in to see you shortly."

"Okay." Penny was only slightly comforted by this. And this would be the first time of many that she chose sleep, in order to rid herself of the pain she felt. She was told she would never be able to walk properly, or run again. She didn't need someone to tell her that she had lost the person she loved most in the world. She could feel Susanna's absence burrowing through her, slicing memories of happiness as it coiled.

"I wanted to tell you, for what it's worth, that you're a miracle. You held on much longer than most people could have." He smiled weakly. Penny blinked and looked down at her hands, raw and covered in ashy skin and oily tar. Momentarily she was thankful for Dr. Martin, who must have been exhausted from saving her life.

"Dr. Martin?" Penny asked, as he stood in the doorway, about to leave.

"Yes, dear?"

"Where's my mother's scarf?"

"Your mother's scarf?" Dr. Martin was unsure what she was referring to.

"It was tied around my leg when I came to the hospital." This was the only thing she remembered from the commotion of the accident.

"Oh, it was full of blood. It was probably thrown away."

"I need it." Her eyes pleaded, as her energy became frail.

"I'll see what I can do."

Penny laid her head back against the pillow and closed her eyes, exhausted. She mumbled "thank you" just loud enough so that Dr. Martin heard it as he walked out the door into the bare halls.

#

When Penny woke later on in the day, Tony was sitting beside her bed, holding her small hand in his. He was watching tenderly as she slept through the most traumatic pain she would ever feel. Penny opened her eyes and turned her head to look at him.

"Hi, Pen." Tony smiled at her, stroking her long black waves of hair, damp and tangled with the terror and torment of the previous day.

"Hi." She smiled, momentarily forgetting where she was.

"I brought you something." Tony reached over to the bedside table and picked up Susanna's red-and-purple scarf. Penny smiled weakly. It was bloodstained, no matter how hard you tried to wash it, but it was a piece of her mother. Penny took it from his hands, smoothing it in her fingers before hugging it to her chest, tears rolling down her pale cheeks. She could still smell her mother in it. Cinnamon.

"I want Mommy." Tears flowed over her chapped lips and into her rough throat, but her voice never croaked, and she never heaved. Tony sensed an anger and a lack of fear that caused him to shift in his chair.

"I want her too, Penny." He paused, reaching over to the bedside table where he had placed the tea he made her. "We have each other." He pressed the tea bag against the inside of the porcelain mug as Susanna had always done, to steep the maximum amount of flavour into the water. Tony, in reality, was so lost that all he could think to do was make tea.

When Penny was able, Tony knew that the best thing for her was to move in with her grandmother. Penny could see the worry and pain in the darkness under Tony's eyes, along with a few fresh wrinkles in his forehead, which she reached up to trace. As Tony climbed into the hospital bed with her, cradling her small body in his, he seemed to draw what remained of her warmth into himself. The only way to protect her would be to keep her away from him. Penny fell asleep again in Tony's arms, with her scraped hands cupped around the warm tea. It had burnt her lips, already withered from the salt of the tears that fell throughout her sleep. A small drop of blood dripped from one of her cuts, down the white porcelain. Tony lay awake, thinking about whether or not he could let her go, if he knew she would live.

#

Penny sat at the kitchen table of her grandmother's house in the middle of New Jersey two weeks later. She flipped her spoon over and over in her hands, casting her reflection up and down. Her grandmother, Winnie, was kind and gentle much like her mother, but Penny was thinking about someone else. Tony had brought her here and told her he needed to go away for a while to protect her. He had promised that he would return when he felt it was safe. Penny had screamed and cried, desperately begging him to stay, but Tony left, driving north along the freeway with the windows open, the cold air blasting the tears away as quickly as they came. Now Penny sulked and couldn't eat her food. Her grandmother did her best to raise her as tenderly as Susanna would have, but Penny's outlook on the world had changed. It had turned dark and cynical at such a young age that Winnie feared there was no path back to the wondrous child she once was. As the seasons passed, the leaves fell and grew, each year turning scarlet red and emulating such warmth despite the fact that they were slowly dying from the exponentially deepening cold.

CHAPTER 5

– Educate –

February 1954, Washington, D.C

After a few months without Susanna, Paul and Tony were lucky they had an obsession with research to continue stumbling over, though they were more motivated now than ever with little hold on their passion. Tony became convinced his drinking amplified his thinking, and Paul struggled to know what to think for himself and of Tony. Both of them relied on sarcasm to stay sane.

Tony and Paul had gathered most of Susanna's belongings and research equipment from the house in Salem. Paul couldn't bring himself to see Penny, and Tony was traumatized from the accident. Their sole intent now was to pretend she didn't exist.

#

Tony's mind snapped from his thoughts, but his eyes didn't. He was staring out the window at the nearly perfect square patch of snow, blocked in by the outer wall of their building and the walls of three others. The space was about four feet by four feet, and if it kept snowing, there would be a perfect rectangular prism up their window, burying them even further in the basement. Two more snows and they would have to close the blinds so they didn't feel claustrophobic.

"Is Jan here?" Tony's gaze still hadn't broken with the crisp white cuboid. Such a clear path the snow had. It didn't even have a choice to make. It just had to fall.

"I think so, but I checked the readings this morning."

"And?"

"When are you going to trust me, Tony?"

"I do." His eyes still hadn't moved.

"Tony?"

"You know how my mind works. I can't stop."

"I know. It's the only thing I can't get you to do."

"Interesting, what can you get me to do?" Tony finally cracked a smile. Paul actually turned to smile this time, but Tony's mind was further away than he thought.

"Is Jan here?"

"Yes." Paul watched Tony stand and stuff his hands in his pockets, one hand still around the neck of a beer bottle, and shuffle toward the door. "Let me know what it says." Tony paused as he opened the door, his knuckles turning white from pushing down the cold steel. He looked back and smiled lightly. Paul smiled back and returned to his papers. He'd wasted enough time being worried.

#

Jan heard a knock on the door and rolled off his dark plum sofa to get it. The stuffing was bulging out of the couch in the same fashion it was from the space between his navel and pants. He scratched his stubble and wiped the sleep from his eyes with his thumb and forefinger. He sighed, wondering, not uncommonly, why he was so dedicated to two guys doing research behind the government's back. He hauled his pants up over himself, and shoved the cotton back into the couch. Jan opened the door to see exactly who he had expected. Nobody else would have been knocking. Nobody else knew who he was.

"Tony, hi. It's eight, my man. Nap time."

"Nice to see you too, Jan."

"Yeah, sure, come in. Nothing's blown up yet in the back." He chuckled and plopped back onto the couch, rolling onto his back.

"Right, so we're doing something wrong."

Jan sat up and stared at him seriously.

"Joke, Jan. That's a joke."

"Right." He yawned and lay back down, arms folding over his rounded stomach. "Would you tell me when you're done back there? I should head home when you do."

"Sure thing."

"Thanks, Tony."

"Thank *you*, Jan." Tony looked at him sincerely and bowed. He felt truly grateful for Jan, who didn't seem to notice. It didn't take long before Tony was back in his own head. He pushed on the brick at the back of Jan's little office and a rectangle about six feet by three feet outlined itself in the brick. Tony, being Tony, had carved it out to fit him. Paul, being Paul, had to duck every time but never complained. Behind the simplest of red brick, lay the prerequisites for something unfathomable, even for Tony's mind.

#

Tony sat slouched in a dark blue plastic chair, legs out in front of him and arms crossed tightly. He was staring at everything and doing nothing. He sat in the middle of the room, his back to the wall where the door was. His and Paul's work was crammed into twenty square feet, bound by dusty red brick that had an odd red stripe in the middle, around the entire perimeter. Two ancient wooden tables that had no doubt been passed down to the janitors because they dated anyone alive in the building, stood against the wall to Tony's right. You could easily tell which was Tony's and which was Paul's, but both were covered with papers, pens, and passion. They had a photo of them when they were about twelve, tinkering with the engine of Mr. Elliott's blue Chevy Eagle sedan thumbtacked on the wall across from him, above the plastic table housing a mess of old machinery they had smuggled from their office, hoping that it wouldn't be missed: infrared machines, satellite imaging machinery, particle trackers, and GPS systems that were on release hold to the public for another twenty or so years. There was also a framed photograph of Susanna. Her face was streaked in light shades of grey, which Tony and Paul vividly remembered as the late summer afternoon light. She leaned against the blue Eagle that Tony and Paul had fixed only because she loved to drive it.

There was a popcorn machine on the other wall under the massive blackboard, a carpet version of chutes and ladders, Scrabble, several decks of cards, several cases of beer that Tony never put in the fridge because they'd be too cold to down. The fridge stood next to them though, holding both biological samples and sample sizes of alcohol left from Tony. Paul always said no one would believe their science if they found out there was tequila next to human blood samples in their fridge. Tony disagreed, arguing that it was their blood and that there was alcohol in it anyway. They were never on the same page about what exactly they were doing. All they knew is that they were obsessed with finding out what happens after death. They had no idea which dots they would connect along the way. They also knew that if they found what they were looking for, they weren't going to share it.

Tony heard the brick scrape across the tile and cocked his head back over the chair to look at Paul leaning against the apparent hole in the wall. His head was slightly ducked because he was too tall for the doorway, which simultaneously made Tony smile and briefly notice his own narcissism. To Tony, Paul was handsome in an irritating way. His perfect hair and vibrant eyes were too blue for this decade and painted an optimism that Tony could never hold. The sky wasn't even this blue, especially in Washington. He was thin, about six foot four now and toned, and as he stood there with his hands on his hips looking at Tony, in a light blue tucked dress shirt and black slacks, Tony realized he still had an aggressive sprinkle of freckles on his nose that hadn't changed since they were kids. Tony looked down at his own lab coat, which he wore over his bare scrawny chest. His dark thick hair was slicked back in alignment with the blackness of his eyes.

"Tony?"

"Yeah?" Tony's sharp jaw tensed. His head was almost out of place on his thin neck.

"It's midnight."

"Is it?" Tony never broke his gaze with everything in front of him.

"Let's go home, and you're waking up Jan."

"You're going to age well." Tony spun in his chair and grinned.

"I'll take it." Paul walked to the corner of the small room, grabbed another chair, and sat on it backwards directly in front of Tony, resting his forearms on the back of it. "Talk to me."

"We should go home. Want a scotch?" Tony asked. Paul stared hard into his eyes. They knew each other too well at this point.

"Here's the thing. We're crazy scientists, right?"

"Speak for yourself." Paul tried to lighten the mood.

"Well, as crazy as one gets in their late twenties."

"And?"

"What if we could pull this off? Susy thought we could." Although they were in a basement of perpetual darkness, they could both feel the heaviness of the thick night settling on the room.

"We're here at midnight, aren't we?" Paul didn't detect how serious Tony was trying to be.

"Fuck, Paul, I'm serious." He stood and spun his chair around to match Paul's and sat down, crossing his arms over the back of the chair.

"Tony." Paul sighed.

"Hear me out."

"Not tonight."

"It wasn't a question. We can do it."

Paul nodded at the floor and shifted his weight in his chair. He looked up and nodded again to show he was really listening. He wasn't convinced by the tone of Tony's voice. He wasn't afraid of him. But he was worried about whether he wanted to expel the energy on this or not. Tony's eyes were bloodshot and watery and he was slightly drunk. Paul was sure he was, but wasn't surprised.

"Okay, so this is what we're working with." Tony stood up and stumbled slightly as he walked to the blackboard and with one sweeping motion wiped it clean with his sleeved forearm, making Paul cringe. He started drawing diagrams frantically, and even after all this time Paul could never decipher any of them.

"Right," Paul said to let him know that he was listening, as Tony's back was still turned.

"Matter can't be created and it can't be destroyed. We cannot simply go nowhere when we die. Something has to go somewhere."

"Precisely. Everyone's trying to figure this out, Tony."

"We're not everyone. Susanna wasn't everyone. That's why we're here."

"Okay, okay, continue."

"Right, so this brought us to something like a soul, constructed of matter, something like electron clouds, which is what we keep looking for," Tony said.

"Well, if there's separation of a soul-type matter from the body, then based on the calculations it has to start happening before the person dies. Because it's not something we necessarily decide," Paul added.

"Which is why we're tracking local people's natural energy emission with the infrareds, satellites, GPS, and started using death certificate data, cemeteries, and terminal hospital records. We just pretend privacy doesn't exist," Tony quipped.

"Right, we randomize and don't know anyone anyway. We're mad scientists. We have no friends."

"You don't have friends."

"Anyway?" Paul asked impatiently.

"People's energies spike before they die."

"But we don't know what causes the spike? Or what it's made of?"

"We know it makes a curve."

"Oh, we do?" Paul's eyebrows raised and he awaited an explanation. Tony drew a bell curve on the blackboard, and a line through it to the right of the middle of the curve.

"It's not a wave, like we thought, it's a predictable curve, of all things."

"What?" Paul was startled. How had they missed this?

"The energy starts to heighten when a person is in their final year of life, it peaks when they die, and levels off. But, it's actually still there afterwards."

Paul's eyes were wide. "How did you figure this out?"

Tony looked at the floor and shoved his hands in his pockets. Paul glared at him. Tony looked up with glossy eyes but no less serious of a look.

"I had to."

"No, you didn't, Tony, she was off limits. We all agreed that…"

"She's the only one I had close enough."

"You couldn't have snuck into a hospital again or something? God, Tony, why?"

"Paul. I had to know."

"No, I'm going home, this is bullshit. You're not the only one who cared about her, you know! What about her parents? You can't tell them."

"You mean, what about you?"

"Yeah, well, she loved you so who are you to betray her?" Paul stood up and headed toward the door. He was furious.

"Paul, please wait. There's more." Tony was begging, and there was a pain in his voice that forced Paul to turn around.

"I picked up her energy signature last night."

"What? Where? What the hell, Tony? She's been dead for almost two months!"

"I picked it up in a child. But it's not strong."

"What?"

"Yeah. I don't know either."

"So what you're telling me, is we know that this energy is transferred somehow, and to whom it is transferred to."

"Precisely."

Paul shook his head. "We're in trouble now, Tony."

"Honestly, I could have told you we would be ten years ago."

#

Tony and Paul fell into frantic rounds of drinking and emotional outbursts the rest of the night. Fits of calculations lined the walls in white chalk once they ran out of room on the blackboard. They fell asleep at their work and woke late into the morning because light couldn't get through solid brick.

When Paul stirred, Tony was at his desk already, scribbling thoughts down. He was one of those people whose ideas came to him in the three hours of sleep he rarely got.

"Did we get anywhere or were you too drunk?" Paul was laying on his back and smiled at the ceiling. "Oh shit! Jan! Did he get home?"

"You were too drunk, I'm better drunk. We know this. And he's not here, so I suppose so."

"Tony, what the fuck."

"What?"

"Can we just talk about all this before we blindly dive into it again?"

"Yeah, we figured out some cool shit. Rather, I did, didn't I?"

"What does that mean?"

"Means what you think it means."

"Screw you."

"You smell, you know?"

"I'm sure you do too. Your arrogance wreaks."

"I'm on to something. Come back later."

"Oh, so I don't even get to know anymore. You don't want to share? Can I not help?"

"No, you can't."

"All right, fine. I'm going to that bagel place on the corner. You come when you feel like we're on the same level again."

"We are."

"Right."

When Tony looked up and turned around Paul was already standing by the door.

"I'm sorry. You can have thirty per cent of the credit." Tony smirked.

"Right, well I get seventy per cent of the food then."

"Fine with me."

"And seventy per cent of the alcohol."

"Not so fine." Tony stood up and picked up a shirt off the floor. They walked to Jimmy's Cafe a few blocks west in the biting cold of the morning, without speaking a word.

#

Tony sat staring at his bagel and coffee, deep in thought. Paul had been shoving his face with eggs, pancakes, and bacon for the past half hour and Tony hadn't said a word or touched a morsel of food. Paul was watching him, waiting for the moment when he was going to erupt into verbal diarrhea, begging, most likely with "Here's the thing."

"Here's the thing."

"I'm listening."

Tony sat back against the plastic red booth and crossed his arms, looking up at the light fixture above their table. "Why is this on? The fucking sun's up." He reached up and unscrewed the light bulb from the fixture, got up, and threw it in the trash and sat back down.

"Here's the thing."

Paul nodded, eyes wide.

"What do we use our memories for?"

"Huh? Our memories?"

"Yeah. We use them to remember things. Lame."

"Oh God, Tony, where is this going?"

"I just think it's bull. What do we use our memories for?"

"Uh, besides remembering things, I haven't a clue."

"We have vivid memories of Susy, right? Hence last night."

Paul gulped and looked down, clenching his jaw. "Well yours might be more vivid than mine."

"Beside the point." Tony's stare was eerie and Paul actually felt uncomfortable, shifting his weight and resting his chin on his hands on the table.

"Go ahead."

"Where do we store memories? Hippo-something-us, right? That part of the brain Susy talked about a lot."

"Yeah, sure, that. The *hippocampus*, Tony."

"Okay, so what if memories equal matter?" Which he wrote with his finger on the table.

"Of course memories matter, what are you getting at?"

"I mean, what if memories *are* matter, kind of?"

Paul raised his eyebrows.

"A soul has to be a complex reconstruction of the mind's experience, but what if we're looking for something slightly different. What if we are looking for a sort of essence of someone? A reconstruction of their memories instead of a soul?"

Paul stared at Tony as if his eyes were listening.

"Let's call it an essence, and let's say this essence becomes increasingly visible and detectable before death, following the energy curve we found. It sticks around for a bit at the peak, and then starts to fade. It's a full bell curve, because the essence is flowing…"

"To someone else." Paul sat back, nodding.

"And just like that, the pathway to another human is formed, but a few questions arise. First, how do we check that? We look for energy curves that match at specific points — ones that fade while another picks up, and with the same signature and composition. Essentially, someone dying and someone expecting a child. Second, think about this. If we think of light years, and how the light we see from stars today was actually omitted millions, maybe billions of years ago, then wouldn't there be data we could pick up from an essence, built of memories and thoughts constructed by sound and light, from the past?"

"I don't follow. Isn't that obvious?"

Tony paused for a moment, searching for another way to verbalize what was in his mind.

"What if memories, once packaged in these essences, are just energy? If they are light and sound energy, then we could access them, hypothetically. We could access someone's memories and figure out what precisely determines who their essence is passed to. It's simple cause and effect."

"Like time travel? Tony, come on."

"We've come this far."

"How would that even be possible?"

"Finish shoving your face and I'll show you. I'm also not fond of letting any of this info slip."

"What? The magical realism in your head?" Paul was sitting back against the booth now, his hands folded on top of his head. He held an interrogative gaze. "Tony, what are you thinking? We have a great job, a half-decent apartment in the city, and you want to go off on this tangent because something happened with Susanna and our parents? We've already messed around too much. I miss her too, but we can't bring her back."

"No, we can't, but I want to meet her successor. What if God or some higher being sees specific memories and experiences, packages them into these essences and sends them to where they are needed, or will be free or something? We could tap into that!"

"And who's ass is this on if things go awry?"

"Both of us?"

"Absolutely not."

"Just let me explain everything to you. It's in my head I just need to write it down, fiddle with it."

"That's what I'm afraid of."

"Paul, we could do something here and I think I know how to do it. I know you want to and you can't always be better safe than sorry."

Paul sat forward and raised his voice a little, elbows on the table and hands motioning frantically. "Yes, I absolutely can. And what makes you think the U.S. government won't get a hold of this? Is this something we really want to know? This could become a shit show and you and I would be centre stage."

"It's not going to get anywhere."

"Bloody hell, Tony."

Tony reached across and grabbed Paul's coffee, downing the rest of it. "We don't have to tell them yet."

"Oh because we can keep a secret operation going indefinitely in the janitor's office of one of the most secretive research buildings in the world. Honestly, I feel like they already know."

"Paul, nobody checks in on our broom closet office building. We're doing the scraps of work for them that nobody wants to do. We're too young. We have too much hope left. I want to do something with it before my liver fails or floods with alcohol. Do you trust me?"

Paul sat back again, and looked out the window at the mounds of snow in the parking lot.

"Paul." There was a long pause and Tony looked away. They both saw a blue Chevy drive up and park outside the cafe.

"Sometimes I wish I didn't, Tony."

CHAPTER 6

– Learn –

March 1954, Washington, D.C.

Tony and Paul sat beside one another across from what was the most obnoxiously big desk they thought they had ever seen, waiting for Charles Wilson, the secretary of defence. They had argued the entire walk there about how they were going to spin their small side experiment in a way that wouldn't get them thrown in jail. Paul seemed to think things would have gone better in the UK, and Tony was too optimistic about where they were now, sitting in this decorated office that made them wonder why they even bothered. Each wall seemed to be coated in frames of stamped and signed papers of congratulations and recognition, though you could tell that the room had hardly been used. The floor was a patriotic-blue carpet. Tony had always thought carpet was impractical and Paul would answer, saying it was only because he was inclined to spill dark liquor. The softness of the endless woodwork spoke for itself. So much was absorbed in this room.

"You're not special because you drink tequila," Tony would usually snap back at him, but today, the two didn't bicker. They sat in silence, squinting at the grid of tiny locked drawers on the front of the desk, which screamed suspicion.

Paul was sitting upright, hugging his briefcase. Tony, despite where he was, was still slouched in his chair with his arms crossed. The usual blank stare was streaked in ink across his face. Only when he heard the door behind him open, did he sit up. He only stood when he saw Paul was standing.

"Gentlemen," the secretary said sternly, nodding his head in their direction, "they tell me you have something for me?"

Tony and Paul looked at each other. They definitely didn't have something *for* him. They had something that they'd been trying to hide from him, until they got caught. Neither of them said a word. They had agreed they'd only say what they needed to.

"Remind me where you work again?" Wilson asked. It was alarming how calm he was.

"They work for me," Mark Jones replied sternly, walking briskly into the room behind them. "They are my interns. They're working on NASA, sir, as astrophysicists. It doesn't seem to be enough for them though — working on potentially one of the biggest projects in history."

"Well, we haven't had a raise since we got here years ago," Tony replied mockingly. Mark sneered at him. In his mid-thirties, Mark had light brown, slightly thinned hair and a personality to match. He had the demeanour of a supremacist asshole with not much substance, literally and for his arguments. Under Forrestal and President Truman, he was working on the beginning stages of what would be the National Aeronautics and Space Administration Act in 1958. Truman had agreed to chase research in rocketry and upper atmospheric sciences. Supposedly this would ensure America was leading in technology. As one of the lead researchers, he'd hired Tony and Paul to do some of the mechanics. Tony and Paul had something different in mind, equal parts selfish and well-intentioned.

Tony cleared his throat. "Allow us to explain, please."

"And why exactly should I listen to two twenty-something-year-old interns who can't take orders?" Wilson replied monotonically. He looked at them as though they were children, ready to be sent off with a warning. Tony took notice of the fact that he didn't expect much from their not-so-small side project.

"With all due respect, sir, we did follow all of Mark's orders. We simply added on a few of our own and gave them to ourselves," Tony said more confidently than he expected. "This has nothing to do with Mark. He didn't think of any of it."

Mark's eyes raised at Tony's boldness.

"You have ten minutes of my time." Wilson sat down across from them at the huge desk, folding his hands in front of him. Charles Wilson was an average-looking man with a relatively friendly face. He was in his early sixties but looked much older. He had minimal hair left and his skin was pale and wrinkled in waves like the sand beneath the water where you can't touch.

Tony looked at Paul who nodded at him to do the talking, which Paul had never been good at. They both paused for a split second on the confliction between protecting themselves and hiding what they knew might be tampered with in the wrong way. Much of what made human life so intriguing was what wasn't known, and understanding that there was much that should remain unknown. Tony tried to maintain his confident charisma, taking a deep breath before he spoke.

"All right. As was mentioned so kindly, we are astrophysicists working mechanics for the upper atmospheric research sector under Mark Jones, who also has several bosses, mind you. Nonetheless, NASA will be an incredible project, we don't doubt that. We were just motivated by something a little less to do with war." Tony paused and gathered his thoughts in his head, subtly afraid that what he was about to explain might cause another war. "We were thinking more along the lines of existential humanity. We used some of your tech, mostly infrared cameras, satellite tech, GPS, particle precision lasers, telescopes, the whole deal to be honest, to, uh," he paused again, "find out what happens after someone dies."

"Oh, well in that case, by all means please enlighten us," Mark replied sarcastically, his stare still relentless.

"I will," Tony replied confidently, matching his tone. He had no regard for the fact that Mark Jones was his boss. In the moment he wanted to prove that the opposite could be true. His ego got the best of him. Paul tried to grab his arm, but Tony pulled it away.

"We understand that matter cannot be created or destroyed. And we understand that through infrared images the brain creates the most energy in the body. This brought Paul and I to wonder if the brain essentially houses a type of soul, or an essence of who someone was, if you will. After you die, this energy simply cannot disappear, so we started looking for it in the atmosphere around people who have died. What we found was astonishing. We found that close to a person's death, specifically within a year, the energy that their brain creates heightens and remains heightened for a few days after they pass."

"Okay, so their brain is still mildly active, that means absolutely nothing. And you've breached privacy."

"Ah, but you see, not only does this energy heighten but it gradually dissipates from the body, as if the universe, or God, or whoever, somehow knows the body has expired its time. We studied the makeup of the energy, which we found is slightly different for every person. We took one person's energy and did a worldwide search for the same energy packet and picked it up in a fetus. It's sort of like epigenetics being hereditary — not a modification of genes, but an alteration of their expression. Once we realized this, we looked at multiple subjects and found that we can pick up the energies of people who are about to die as well as where that energy is going. We're calling them essences."

"Why essence and not energy?" Wilson asked intently. His eyes were wide in anticipation of the potential this held. He thought of the wars and the country's fear of future ones. Paul cringed. Tony didn't notice.

"Well there's more, sir," Tony replied. Paul dug his nails into Tony's arm, which he didn't seem to feel. If they were going to conceal anything it was what Tony was about to say.

"Do you have ten more minutes?" Tony smirked over at Mark.

"I have all the time you need, Crypt."

"Well, you see, when we recently looked more deeply into what these energies are made of, they weren't just energy. Much of the person is maintained. The essences are just what they sound like — the essence of the person. They are composed of memories."

"Memories?"

"Yes, memories. Memories and experiences through a state of astral projection, which we think we can access. Of course, that's the layman's explanation."

"You mean to say that someone can theoretically enter someone else's essence and experience their memories as if they were there?" Mark asked sarcastically.

"Yes, that's exactly what I mean. There's a caveat though. The person has to be alive and we can't access past essences inside someone. Those are dormant somewhere and we don't know where they are stored. We can only access the essence of a person alive today, and only when they are within one year of their preordained death."

"This is lunacy," Mark replied to Wilson.

"I don't suppose you've discovered anything of the sort, Mark?" Tony asked.

"No, because it's impossible."

"Why don't we give them a chance to show us and then decide, Mark. We can fund it on a bigger scale," Wilson replied calmly but insistently. Paul could feel his heartbeat in his hands gripping his arms. He was furious.

Mark rolled his head back and then shook it in disapproval at the floor.

"That's the trouble. The only way to connect two essences is for them both to be near death, sir," Tony replied.

"You can't artificially impose it?" Wilson asked.

"Not yet, sir. It would involve astral projection of a sort. We need to do more research."

"Do you need anything to be able to do it?"

"Time travel? A miracle? I'm not sure."

"We'll work on that," Wilson replied confidently.

"How did you come across this idea? You have a personal stake in researching all of this?" Mark cut in, staring coldly at both Tony and Paul.

Tony and Paul looked at one another and Paul answered, "No, sir, simply interest."

"He speaks! What about you, Tony?" Mark replied irritatingly.

"Nope, nothing I can think of, Mark! Why, were you expecting there to be a reason?" Tony asked coolly. He wondered what Mark's push for this answer meant. His stomach felt like a sandbag as the image of Susanna's lifeless body floated through his mind as effortlessly as the car had.

"No, it would just be interesting to know, as passion drives most great discoveries, doesn't it?"

"I suppose it does, Dr. Jones," Tony answered. "I'd like to know what it is that drives what happens to them afterwards," he added briskly. There was a rawness in his voice that Paul didn't recognize.

"Do you have a name for this project?" Wilson interrupted, asking both Tony and Paul.

"Um, Penelope. Project Penelope," Tony answered without thinking. He looked at the floor, alarmed by what he had just done. Paul stared at him in horror.

"We'll talk about this further and decide on a course of action, research, implementation, etc. But for now we need to look at the privacy breach and possible concerns elsewhere. You did steal government equipment," Wilson answered matter-of-factly.

"True, but it's his, so how much weight does that hold?" Tony replied, nodding to Mark.

Wilson frowned. "You're not special, Crypt."

#

A few weeks after their conversation, Tony strode after Mark down the hallways of their office building, past Jan's office.

"You can't just take our life's work and do all this bullshit with it, Mark!" Tony yelled down the hall, barging angrily into his office and gripping the door before Mark shut it. Tony and Paul had discovered something, but they had no say or input on how to use it. Unintentionally, they gave full agency to political and military power to make the decision, and Tony hated himself for not having known how to better control his ego.

"It is government property now, Tony. There's not much I can do. You used intel and technology to do your illegal little side experiment. You really should be in jail."

"For getting my foot in the door of the world's biggest mystery?"

"Partially. You've hardly tested anything yet and you have no idea what you're going to do with it! It's a good thing we caught you when we did. The science is brilliant, but let us do the decision making. We're not going to let you do that."

"I can't imagine why! You're going make a selfish decision because you're afraid! A toothpick could predict what you're going to do! You're going to manipulate people's essence trajectories and the next fucking generation just because you can! These are people's memories, Mark! You're playing God!"

"That's what people with power do, Crypt. Look at yourself. Paul isn't even here and I'd bet you didn't even tell him."

"No, not all of them. Just cowards. And this whole aggressive and argumentative mantra isn't really his cup of tea, if I'm being honest. We won't be any part of this. We won't help you."

"The Sifting Project wasn't my decision, all right? It actually wasn't really Charles's either, or NASA's. It's a decision to prevent a third war. Isn't that of any importance to you?"

"So it's called the Sifting Project now? What are you planning to do? Sift through people's memories for what you want to keep quiet? Or for what you like? Stop people from dying or kill them early? You can't prevent a war by controlling people's minds. That is how you *start* a goddamn war, Mark!"

"Nobody will know. You're a kid, Tony. You listen and answer to us. You want the people in your life to be safe? Do as we say or things will get messy. Who's to say they already aren't. There was a girl, right?"

"Don't you dare bring her into this, Mark. She had nothing to do with it. We're done. Fuck off and stay the hell away from us." Tony pressed his teeth together.

"We? You don't really get any say, Tony. It's do this or go to jail. This is admirable, important work that you'd be doing for us. We're fully funding it, giving you neuroscientists and scalable equipment to access all essences and scan for the ones we need. Your continued research on this for the rest of your life will keep you out of jail, do you understand?"

Tony leaned against the wall with his hands in his pockets. He bit into his bottom lip to stop himself from saying anything else. Mark collected his things off of his desk and stormed out of the office. For the first time in his life, Tony really didn't know what the right thing to do was, and he struggled with the idea that his decision to keep Penny, himself, and his best friend safe rivalled humanity's best interest. As per usual, those with power were looking to use something that could save the world for their temporary benefit. Tony drove back to the apartment. He needed to think, but wanted to speed, so he drove along every back road, deliberating how he was going to start the conversation with Paul.

#

A few days later, Tony and Paul were forced to move into a home in the township of Kingston, New Jersey, far away from any significant population, and conduct their research. For their own freedom, they developed the technology to do what they had theorized. They developed a way to pinpoint the exact moment when someone dies, based on the essence trajectories and the curve of their energy composition. They designed a way to functionally visualize the actual memories and content in essences. They were instructed to locate the memory threads which most strongly predicted the natural course of an essence. To their dismay, the Sifting Project came to full fruition when Tony and Paul finalized an astral projection machine, which enabled government-recruited Sifters to sift targeted memories. Sifters sought to manipulate memories enough to change the essence's trajectory favourably, stop someone from dying, or eliminate them sooner. Often, this process involved the assassination of the person in specified memories, which permanently deletes those memories, and severs their contribution to the essence's natural trajectory, creating the ability to form a new one.

In the twenty-five years that followed, Tony and Paul gave lectures about the Sifting Project and briefed the recruited Sifters who would follow these orders. They taught astrophysics at Princeton University as a cover, and went through the motions of their life for the next twenty-five years, living in fear, anger, annoyance, and limited agency. Lists of people who the government wanted sifted, consistently floated through the mail to their home. Tony and Paul tracked these people's essences and mocked up the manipulation paths requested. The natural flow of essences was disturbed on a scale that even Tony and Paul didn't understand, and though it was wrong, it wasn't this that scared them. It was the possibility of unlocking the memories in essences further back, dormant in people's minds. This is why there was such an effort to keep everything internal — God forbid knowledge, stories, and experiences filtered through different hands than they were meant to.

Tony punched the walls as he wrote reports for the Sifters on how to tamper with specific memories enough to change an essence's trajectory. Nepotism and nationalism reigned, and Tony and Paul's hearts were slowly being grated like cheese, as Sifters were sent into specific memories to alter the paths of the essences. Changing memories changed the energy signature irreversibly — it could stop someone from dying, or ensure that essences were passed to someone favourable.

Tony and Paul had suspected these things, though they never planned to act on them. They didn't understand why the patterns of essences existed in the first place and they hoped they never would. The paths that essences naturally followed weren't up to them, though, there had to be a reason — a landscape of story sharing and experience that was better left alone. They were playing God now, and when you play God, He tends to play back, as the wars had demonstrated time and time again. Tony and Paul lived solemnly, growing closer together despite their differences. The government's handprints covered their research, documents, and all of the technology that they built but couldn't keep. The very first astral projection machine sat collecting dust in the corner of their office in Kingston. Nothing was theirs anymore. They were numb enough to forget Susanna and Penny, finding an eerie familiarity in being all each other had.

CHAPTER 7

– Embrace –

Summer 1969, Chester, New Jersey

B eck sat at the kitchen island with his chin resting on his forearms, knuckles knocking the dull grey marble that had been cratered by burns from overflowing hot candles. His eyes, two swirling pools of late-night ocean, held a firm gaze with the television mounted above the fridge. A polished red stripe lined the skyline, below a navy sky. The Frosted Flakes, milk jug, and a bowl, used three times by this point, were sitting to his left. At fifteen, nearly sixteen, Beck stood almost six feet, didn't play any sports, resembled an ironing board and was exceedingly, though mysteriously, bright. Quietly, in jeans and armed with a cold stare, Beck held the highest GPA in his school unbeknownst to any of his classmates. He had been told he resembled Dennis Wilson, though his heart chambers were securely locked from his sleeves.

It was nearly 11 p.m. and his aunt Mary had long gone to bed. He was awaiting one of the biggest events in history. Beck loved his aunt Mary but he had the television on full volume, as if more sound would spill the news out at its speed. The black, white, and grey fuzz hardly depicted anything worth watching on the small mint green set mounted in the corner above the fridge, maroon cupboards and painfully off-white walls. They had been stained by blotches of smoke columns and bathed in the scents of Mary's cooking. There must have been a time when they looked less like worn-out lipstick. Why his aunt had the television mounted way up there he never understood.

Under Beck's right elbow was a notebook painted in scribbled sketches of rockets, astrophysics research, and anything he could make note of and get his hands on. As the screen began to scrape into the sounds of a broadcast, he perched his pencil between his fore and middle finger and tapped it off the table impatiently. He noticed the dissipating red sky out the window, illuminating the kitchen like a darkroom. Beck had few friends besides aunt Mary's children, who were much younger than him. For the past ten years he had helped look after them and grown to adore them. Mary always said he was her guardian angel and the more Beck thought about it now that he was older, the more he realized that she might be his. Around the time Mary went through her much needed divorce and was left with her two young children, who were one and three at the time, both her and Beck lost the most wonderful family in the world. Beck's parents had planned to take in Mary and her children until she had rekindled her life, but were killed in a car crash coming back from their weekly dinner together downtown.

Beck was six. Laying in space-themed sheets pulled up to his nose on an abnormally cold winter night, he was awake much longer than usual and was trying desperately to fall asleep. He closed his eyes, which darted like a stormy ocean under his eyelids, and thought of the bright red sunrise he'd watched with his mom that morning. He was sure he hadn't heard his mother and father come in after he'd climbed into bed, because he always looked for the shadows of their footsteps beside his door as they passed it, heading down the hall to the bathroom. He awaited the click of his mother's heels and clunk of his father's dress shoes on the tile floor, which finally soothed him into sleep. He knew that if neither of them left the bathroom, he could expect smiles and pancakes the next morning. He also usually heard his babysitter, Gabby, who had been studying in the dimly lit, cozy kitchen booth just down the hall of his parent's modest home. He liked hearing the pages of her books make that thick flop as their spines closed around them. When she closed each one, Beck's drawings on the fridge ruffled. He added a new one almost every week, as a continuation of the last, like a comic: "The adventures of Beck and Binta." Binta was Gabby's middle name, which Beck loved. He loved the sound of their names together. Binta always hummed softly while she carefully packaged each book back into her bag, switched off the rust-bucket stove that she left on to keep warm and clicked off the lights. He usually fell asleep by the time her humming ceased, as she exited calmly and quietly through the back door, where she parked her white-and-blue bicycle against the old fence that Beck had never seen fully painted. Beck was sure he had heard none of that tonight.

This was when he heard screams of horror and sobbing from the kitchen. Binta was shrieking into the receiver of the telephone, her hand clasped over her mouth trying to muffle the sounds of her terrorized panic. Little Beck didn't move. He lay perfectly still, hoping he was only dreaming. He listened to Binta's quiet tears and sobbing for another few minutes, wondering if he'd use any of his own. When she finally came down the hall to Beck's room, her eyes rolled over a wide-eyed child who she didn't know how to comfort.

"Beck, honey, I'm so sorry."

"Where's Mommy and Daddy?" Beck whispered. Binta dropped to her knees and covered her face, unable to hold back her tears. Beck climbed out of bed and nestled his small body into her arms. They sat in the dark room, almost as dark and removed as deep space, curled around one another for what felt like an eternity before blue-and-red lights flashed softly into the room. It was almost a sort of purple. Beck pictured his mother in her favourite purple peony dress.

Nearly ten years later, Beck sat at Mary's kitchen table now wondering how Binta was. Sometimes he saw notes from her and purple peonies left at his parent's grave, but he had hardly seen her since that day. She had been older and probably remembered more of them. He wondered about talking to her. Beck was snapped from his thoughts by the explosion of smoke flashing across the television. He scrambled to open his notebook and grabbed his pen. The ship was landing on the moon.

#

In the winter of 1969, Penny spent hours at the beach until her cheeks were hot with cold, watching the destruction of the lapping waves wreaking havoc in the sand. Penny loved her grandmother, but she would never say it. The words never made it from her throat. She did appreciate the compassionate soul who comforted her through her mood swings and cushioned her hatred for the world. Penny tried desperately to be pleasant, and her efforts didn't go unnoticed.

Penny's heart curled in on itself the older she got. She fostered a carefree, introspective pessimism, though she was never outwardly contemptuous. She reminded her grandmother of Tony more and more every day, but of course this wasn't ever a topic of conversation. Penny sought to erase Tony from her mind. She had once admired, loved, and deeply respected Tony in a way she didn't understand, perhaps rooted in how she longed for a father. She could no longer bear to hear him in her head or feel the dust of his influence collecting in her heart. That was the thing about dust — it collected. He'd left when she needed him most.

#

"Penny, dear?" Winnie called, holding a few groceries and hanging her keys on the hook by the door. She glanced down to take her boots off, noticing the small etches in the wood panels, about three feet from the floor. When Penny was little, she marvelled in the fact that the house was a canvas, carving stories into its wooden walls. The house was old and showed its age, but Winnie smiled longingly at the extra character Penny had given it.

"Penny? I found some of that blueberry tea you like!" Winnie's voice was soft and raspy, so much so that the pouring rain drowned her calls. She walked carefully down the dark hallway, which even on the sunniest days hardly let light in. Penny's door was closed. Winnie hesitated a moment before she knocked.

"Penny?" There was no response. Winnie opened the door slightly, turning the knob so as not to make a noise. Penny was asleep in her bed, with a few magazines and books. The window was cracked open, just enough so that she could hear the rain deadening against the stone exterior of the house, the damp absorbing into it, forming a deeper shade of grey.

Winnie sighed, glancing around the room — a dismal theatre of crushed hope. On her bed, copies of *The Dial*, *Aurora Leigh*, and *The Colour Out of Space* lay open and heavily annotated. Her walls were spotted with tiny forget-me-nots, along with probably one hundred handwritten passages from books and quotes by authors Winnie hadn't heard of. Many had names she couldn't pronounce. Beneath each passage or quote was the name of the author, and a note which explained its pronunciation. Winnie never understood Penny's habits — she followed the army of stories and memories inside her which she had been taught, unaware that they were few in numbers compared to the ones Penny sought to unlock. Winnie sighed and stroked Penny's hair. *God, you write the most troublesome tests,* she thought. She reached down to the end of the bed and pulled a quilt up over Penny's shivering body. Winnie paused on one corner of the quilt. It was composed of four poorly sewn patches, made from four of the dresses Penny had outgrown. Even in the quilt, they breathed memories. Tony had made it for her for Christmas the year Susanna died. He gave it to Penny the day he left her. Since then, Penny sewed on new patches of memories. She was desperately afraid of forgetting, though she wanted to. Her truth was in the past, and the quilt allowed her to keep it there.

#

Penny tumbled seamlessly into writing early in high school when her other grades looked grim. She never lost her thoughtfulness, but her mind turned it over differently in loneliness. She wasn't always sure she chose to be alone either. She found it fascinating thinking about the fulcrum that her mind rested on — a delicate line between light and dark at 4 p.m. in the winter. From which her actions were rooted, she was unsure. She feared having nothing to do in her brain, and gave what was left of her heart to writing and noticing a little more each day. It was almost as if her critical mind could piece together and perfect the imperfection and loss that defined her life. She longed for winter in its harshness and ability to glaciate. Though ink was permanent, Penny set her manuscripts on the frozen wood of the windowsill in February, to freeze the ink even further into time.

As she got older, she found, somewhat irritatingly, that the people around her breathed for complex beauty, not that complexity was anything to be understood at this moment. Perhaps there would be a moment when the complexity of simplicity would spill violently out in white-and-sage waves for her, but until then she preferred her own lens. The deficit of colour was illuminating. She understood the eye as being naturally drawn to colours, but not often enough to the simple visual cues and experiences that they paint. *Like love*, she thought. She thought of the last movie she saw. She contemplated what, precisely, she remembered from it — characters, relationships, raw humanity only tinted by the darkness of black and the blinding of white. She did not consider that perhaps the lead lady's dress was a wealthy depth of purple. It was simply like everyone else's. *So*, she thought, *I'm left to judge the raw beauty of her character*. When she wrote, she introduced herself to her characters as a complicated kind of simple each time. She didn't loathe the able bodied. She didn't want to inspire. She didn't want to be saved. She didn't want to overcome anything. She just wanted to *be*, and she wrote and observed the world as if she was. But she also didn't trust the parts of herself that she needed to unlock to heal.

#

In December of 1973, in the only small diner in downtown Chester, New Jersey, Becker Brooks sat across from Binta Lane, who was home from medical school for the Christmas break. They both stared down at their hands, which were clasped tightly around their coffees. It was another uncharacteristically cold winter, and in the spirit of the holidays Binta had phoned Beck. It had been years and she had been thinking about him, wondering how he was faring and how he had grown. She also knew he would be old enough now to talk and perhaps might want to. Beck recognized her immediately, and although he thought her shimmery brown ringlets, caramel ribbon skin, and caffeinated eyes were beautiful, he had never seen her romantically. He'd always admired her presence and her mind, and was now acutely aware that others didn't. When they played Candy Land as kids, he drew a princess card for her. He remembered her softness, which she still carried. He knew he'd always care about her, as she would him. She'd matured into a grace and intelligence that she'd always had. Binta, on the other hand didn't recognize Beck at all when she first walked in, only catching his uniquely dark blue eyes when he looked up under his grey hoodie and dark baseball cap. They both teared up and embraced in a long, warm hug, as if to say, "I'm here, and I've got you, just like I did that night." But both felt the eyes on them.

"Binta, we can go somewhere else?" Beck said.

"We could, but that's giving them what they want, isn't it?"

"I can't just sit here though."

"*You* can't?"

"No, sorry, that's not what I meant. I mean, it's always bothered me. Even when we were kids. I don't want to be a silent coward."

Binta smiled. "You don't have to be. Right now, let's get to know each other again. After, what you choose to stand for is up to you."

"I want to stand up for you."

"Don't just stand up for me because I'm your friend. Stand up for everyone."

Beck nodded, and folded his hands in his lap, looking down, unsure what to say next.

"Think about it this way. I don't need you to speak for me. I've got this shit. I need you to help configure a life where I can just live, you know? Live without fear because of what I look like. Thanks for not pretending it doesn't exist though. It means a lot."

Beck nodded again, and looked up smiling. He felt safe with Binta. He always had. He tried to commit this moment to memory. A sign behind Binta read: "Our souls are made of music and light." *Music and light*, Beck thought. Is it better to see or listen?

#

After exhausting everything that was currently going on in their lives, Beck learned that Binta was attending medical school at Oxford and had made friends with a girl who she met at the library studying. Binta joked that if he were a little older, Beck should totally go for her. Beck assured Binta that he wasn't really interested, which surprised her.

"What are you interested in, then? You're almost twenty." Her eyebrows were raised as she took a sip of her coffee.

Beck looked down and laughed, lifting his fingers away and back to the cup to feel its warmth again. "Well, I suppose space."

"Oh, isn't everyone?"

"Yeah, I'm really interested in all the science, I guess. Big, grey, dented rocks. I'm studying them in college."

Binta laughed, glancing at the NASA emblem on Beck's hat. "There's always more to them than what they look like."

"That's why I like them." He still hadn't looked up.

"Beck?"

"Hm?"

"Are you okay? Really? How are you? There's not a day that goes by that I don't worry about you."

"So does Mary."

"Mary?"

"My aunt."

"Right, she had two boys too?"

"Yeah."

"Beck, would you look at me, please?"

He looked up into her eyes. "I'm fine, Binta. I miss them. But I'm okay."

"I don't believe you."

"Well I am." He crossed his arms firmly and stared at her.

"Such a teenager now, huh, Becker Brooks?"

"At least I'm not old."

"Watch it!"

Beck smiled, and Binta looked back at him, still concerned. She put her arm up abruptly to call the server, who hustled over. "Yes, ma'am?"

"Hi, yes, um, could I get two slices of blueberry pie, please?"

"You want it warmed? With ice cream?"

Binta looked at Beck, smiling as she spoke. "His slice warmed with chocolate, mine warm with vanilla, thanks!"

"Sure." She hustled away, folding up her notebook and shoving it in her apron pocket.

"You remembered," Beck said.

"Won't ever forget it. Chocolate ice cream and blueberry pie. Disgusting."

They talked for a few more hours before they headed out, stomachs warm and full. It was just starting to get dark. They decided to walk by the Brooks' old house, which had new tenants now, but hadn't changed much. They stood and admired its warmth from the dimly lit street, both trying to conceal their tears. The fence had been painted and the house had green shutters now, on which the snow perched perfectly. The house almost looked like a snow-dusted evergreen. Binta leaned her head on Beck's shoulder, and they linked arms as the snow began to fall faster, like streaks of white paint under warm street-light brushes. She put her hands in her pockets, her fingers wrapping around her cold plastic lab badge. Two small tears welled in her tear ducts. She wondered if Beck ever knew. In Mr. and Mrs. Brooks' will, a savings account had been left to Binta for college.

"You okay?" Beck's voice was raspy from the cold.

"Oh, yeah, I was just thinking." She sniffled and wiped away her tears. "Did you know they helped me pay for Oxford?"

"Yeah, I did." Beck smiled. "I added in all three quarters from my piggy bank."

Binta laughed. "I'm honoured." There was a long pause, as they both watched the Christmas lights on the house come on. "I didn't even know until they died."

"I know, it's okay."

"You're good like them, you know. I see so much of them in you. Don't let this world convince you that you're not capable and keep you from doing what's right."

"I'll do my best."

"Nope, you promise me right now."

"I promise."

"Good." She squeezed his arm tight.

#

They promised to keep in touch, and did for the next few years that followed, always meeting up to have pie and coffee and pay a visit to the house that once illuminated how simple and ample happiness could be.

They needed the reminder that warmth still existed in the chaos of the new world. Soon, Binta was a doctor living in San Jose, California. Beck was nearly finished university, locally at Princeton. Occasional phone calls were far and few between, until Binta had terminal cancer in 1975. As if the suddenness of loss hadn't hit him hard enough the first time, Beck's heart cracked in places he didn't think it could. He was stripped of any sense of safety and protection he had left.

For weeks, he didn't go to see Binta. If he didn't go, maybe she couldn't. Maybe only hearing was less painful than seeing.

#

As Beck sat outside the hospital room, shivering in the icy air conditioning, he gripped the stems of a bouquet of gladiolus perennials in his hands. He almost couldn't bring himself to walk in the door.

"Mr. Brooks? Gabrielle can see you now." The nurse peaked her head out of the doorway. The mint green colour of her smock almost made him gag. Beck stood and walked in gingerly, stopping in the doorway to prepare himself. There she was. Her hair was gone, her skin chapped and cracked, and her eyes weak. He wrung the flower stems in his palms.

"Hey, Binta."

"Hey, Beck."

It was the last time he saw her. A few weeks later, Beck lay uncomfortably on his bare dorm mattress staring at the stippled ceiling, trying to connect the dots in a constellation. His overdue library books, papers, notebooks, and pencils were spewed across the room, along with the bedding he told himself he'd wash that day. He thought of that sign in the coffee shop — the one that read: "Our souls are made of music and light." He gritted his teeth. If this were the case, he wondered where Binta's soul was now. Who decided where it went? It couldn't disappear. He wondered if he could listen for the music of it and see the light of it in someone else. He rolled over onto his side. A hard cardboard corner jammed into his hip bone.

"Fuck." Beck rolled back over and pulled a botany book out from under him. He had borrowed it to look up flowers for Binta in the hospital. Now, he'd use it each time he would visit her grave. He flipped to a bookmarked page. It was the one about perennials, which live intricately choreographed lives above and below the surface of the earth. During warm months, they boast a beautiful flower, while the roots underground prepare for the dark, cold winter. After the first frost, dead flower petals fall and buds crack in the icy wind, while the roots under the cold soil are very much alive, saturated with life and nutrients that they've been storing for this exact moment, and for the next round of life that they will live. Their resilience is unparalleled. Though, with limited nutrients and compassion from the ecosystem, periods of starvation, isolation from the sun, and harm flow through into the generational cycles, uninterrupted unless reset and rebuilt. With plants, it is easy to interrupt and rebuild from the path of trauma. *But humans still choose not to do it.* Ecosystems correct themselves, in a way, but Beck wondered if anyone, or anything, ever tried to correct it elsewhere at mass scale. Perhaps more importantly, he wondered if anyone had tried to stop an attempt to.

CHAPTER 8

– Elevate –

January 1979, Kingston, New Jersey

Paul and Tony had aged. They both sat at their kitchen table across from one another, wondering how yet another year could go by as slowly. The most painful prospect each January brought was helplessly reliving the same year again. Their heads throbbed with the inability to clip the thread of life they were forced to follow based on the past. Paul was reading a damp newspaper with his coffee and Tony was sitting with his arms crossed, tapping his foot anxiously. A full glass of orange juice had been sitting in front of him for two hours.

"Would you stop, please," Paul asked without looking away from what he was reading.

"What?"

"Stop tapping your leg."

"Why? Am I *bothering* you?"

"Yes, Tony, you are."

"And this is new?"

"What is it?" Paul set the paper down over the toast that Tony had made, and took his glasses off, setting them on top of the paper. He folded his hands together over the pile and searched Tony's eyes for what was troubling him.

"You know, you should have gotten married," Tony mumbled.

"Huh?"

"You should have!" He stood and walked to the refrigerator behind him, pulled out the frozen raspberries from the freezer trunk below, and sat back down. He crunched them like chunks of sorbet. Paul watched him, brows raised. He winced slightly, thinking about the icy fruit grinding in Tony's teeth, electrifying the nerves under his gums.

"And why is that?" He frowned, revealing the years lining his face.

"I don't know, we're getting old and grumpy in this house. We've been here for twenty-five years."

"I don't like the idea of you rumbling around in here alone," Paul responded truthfully.

"Maybe that's what I need?"

"No, it most definitely is not," Paul laughed. "You'd be seething around here for a few weeks, forget to eat, and die. May I finish reading now?"

"Not yet. There's more up here." He pointed to the centre of his forehead. Paul was equally thankful for and irritated by the moments when Tony admitted he needed to release his thoughts. Regrettably, Paul still worried about him, knowing that the light and glamour that wove through his mind had more opposites, many of which he did not converse with externally. When Tony got an idea, he felt privileged that it was placed in his hands, allowing it to go viral in his mind in both dark and bright ways. He struggled to follow one or the other based on his own intuition, and thus Paul listened, as perhaps the only one who could sift through what tumbled coarsely out of Tony's mouth.

"All right. I'm listening." Paul reached under his paper and pulled out a piece of pumpernickel toast and grabbed the raspberry jam from the centre of the table. "Would you grab me a knife, before you start, please?"

Tony tilted his chair back on its hind legs and opened the drawer beside the fridge, pulled out a spoon, and tossed it across the table to Paul.

"Tony, I said a knife."

"Spoons work better." Tony smiled, crossing his arms again. He did this when he was nervous.

"Must be an American thing."

"You're not listening, you're eating my jam."

"Sharing."

"Right."

"What are you thinking about at this hour, or since whenever you began your aimless wandering this morning?" Paul had become much calmer and less antagonistic with age. He carefully spooned out the jam, and smoothed it over the toast using the backside of the spoon. The kitchen window behind Paul was open, and the emerald velvet drapes were pinned back against the dark walls. They were the one thing that was left with the house when they moved in and Tony had insisted they keep them. He often sat in the dark hours of the morning with them drawn, waiting for the first streak of light between them to reflect onto the table, and then creep toward him. Without the window open the kitchen was an insidious black box. The wallpaper was black with tiny white-and-green flowers. They were so tiny that neither Tony or Paul could figure out what type they were. The white winter light came in over Paul's back and magnificent shoulders, illuminating the redness of the raspberry jam. The room was accented with the cherry oak wood table, matching cupboards lining the top rim of the whole room, and marble countertops. It was an old house, but the evergreen undertones hid the years of cycling seasons absorbed into the walls. What permeated out was a cross pollination between the past and where the two men sat now. Tony thought that the house might have been a witch's meeting place once. He could picture murky glass bottles of absinth, nightshade, belladonna, and mandrake complemented by a gurgling pot over the open fire, which had since been bricked over. Tony had decided he liked the eeriness. It spoke somehow. It matched the work they did and was filled with fragments of a history that likely didn't breathe far beyond these walls. Lives had been lived here before them. Tony noticed their remnants because he eventually chose to look. For twenty-five years of sinusoidal isolation, he was forced to know himself uncomfortably, in a way that created space for memories and choices that were not his own, nor his to judge. This Monday morning, these were the thoughts that made him think.

Behind Tony was the used fridge and a scraped-up ceramic sink. The series of doorways to the living room, hallways, foyer, and stairs to their basement office looked like a series of inescapable black holes. The window behind Paul looked out over the miles of white hills. Their closest neighbour was about half a mile in the other direction. Tony and Paul didn't teach on Mondays — this was the day that they were supposed to recruit Sifters and Siftees.

"Why are we doing this, Paul?"

"Doing what?" Paul asked, continuing to spread his jam over his toast.

"You know exactly what."

"No, I don't. I think teaching astrophysics at one of the greatest universities in the world, living out here in peace, and the jam lady are wonderful."

"You're zero help."

"I'm supposed to be listening to *you*, I thought."

"All right," Tony replied with a tinge of anger and frustration. "I know you hate what this project has become just as much as I do. Twenty-five years we've been doing this shit and it's wrong. It's very wrong."

"We have this conversation every Monday, Tony."

"I know. And I get angrier every damn time."

"But what else are we going to do?"

"Stop?"

Paul looked up.

"Refuse to do it?" Tony replied to himself.

"Tony, I don't trust them either but this is a legal bind. We can't just run away. They trust us with this now."

"Easy to trust someone you lock away in the middle of nowhere! It's not an honour to be trusted to do what we're doing," Tony raised his voice.

"We teach at Princeton! That's definitely not nowhere!" Paul matched Tony's tone.

Tony sat back, craning his neck up toward the ceiling, which was also painted pitch black.

"We're trapped."

"I don't think we are. Give it time."

"Time, right, why didn't I think of that yet? We've had enough time to think of everything." The two sat in silence. Tony was frustrated by his thoughts.

"There's a battle we have to fight here, Paul. If it's the case that we've been given uniforms to fight in it, then we need to put them on."

"No, it's too much of a risk."

"Risk of what? Our freedom? We can't fuck with fate. There's a point where we have to take the risk. I've reached the point where sitting here compliant and silent is much louder than the voices that we have a hand in silencing. It rings in my ears."

"Tony, we can't put her in danger."

"Paul, we haven't seen Penny since the '50s. How can you sit downstairs every day, see the natural course of an essence's projection, and then document how to dismantle it and change it? We've spent our lives teaching Sifters which memories to target, and how to sever them. The universe or God or someone is trying to create balance and equality with this pattern that existed way before we found it. Essences are collections of memories, experiences, and life. We have to believe that they are sent where they are needed. It's beautiful and incredible and we're fucking with it!"

"It's just control. We can't uproot the system that created it."

"We can. I'll sit in jail. I don't care."

"Tony."

"I don't. And you'll sit in jail with me."

"Yes, I would, and that's what I'm worried about."

They both laughed awkwardly, completely lost for direction.

"C'mon." Paul stood, tucked the newspaper under his arm, took one last bite of his toast, and grabbed his coffee. "We've got work to do."

"I'll be down in a minute. I didn't eat."

"And you probably won't," Paul said, brushing past him, setting his plate beside the sink.

"We just have to do the next right thing, Paul. We have to be loyal to the truth in the past and the one being lived now."

Paul crumpled his newspaper and tossed it in the trash. "For today, that's going downstairs and complying."

"No, it's not," Tony replied, staring blankly out the window. Paul sighed, and left. Tony heard Paul's footsteps on the stairs. With time he'd gotten much heavier on his feet.

#

Tony stayed upstairs for another twenty minutes, staring out at the rolling hills of snow, arms crossed, unsure what to do and unsure of whether or not he could get himself to walk down the stairs. He shivered and realized he was still wearing the t-shirt he slept in. He walked to his bedroom and pulled out a sweater he'd had since he was a teenager. It was hideous but it was warm. As he pulled it over his head he heard muffled cursing through the floorboards. The house was wearing thin, and drafted conversation as it did cold. The stairs to the basement were just to the left of the doorway to his bedroom.

"Everything all right down there?" Tony called from the top of the stairs.

"Um, I think you should come see this," Paul replied anxiously.

"See what?"

"You'll know when you come and see it."

Tony came down the stairs slowly, a familiar plaque forming in his throat.

Paul was sitting at the monitor which tracked essence trajectories. It was a confusing configuration of GPS, satellite, and infrared technology that could track human energy signatures in the atmosphere, specifically those of the brain — essences. The essence trajectories appeared as liquid flowing light, fuzzy on the monitor like elliptical pink strings of frost from one person's location to another. Their motion was fluid, calm, viral, and lyrical, though the beginning and end points were concrete. It was striking to watch, much like galactic interactions, though there wasn't much nuance. Tony's eyes followed one line, concentrated at one end and gradually fading out infinitely, as if the colour were flowing erroneously out into space. Tony walked closer and stood behind him, placing his shaking hands on the back of Paul's chair.

"What the hell?" Tony peered over Paul's shoulder.

"It's going into the atmosphere, and then look, it splits into thousands of curves."

"No, no. That has to be a mistake. Reload it." Tony squinted, focusing hard on what he was seeing. For once, his mind was empty.

"I have, many times, Tony. It has thousands of destinations."

Tony put his hands on his head and began pacing around the room. "My God."

"There, um, there's more."

Tony snapped around. "Who is it?" he demanded.

Paul paused, drawing in a fragmented breath. "It's Penny, Tony."

Tony half fell and half sat on the floor. His head was in his hands. Stunned tears formed in his eyes from holding them open and the ball in his throat choked his voice. "How?" was all he could manage to dislodge.

Paul's eyes were also glossy. "She's on the list."

"What?"

"The list of people we are supposed to report on and send to Mark. She's on the list."

"Why?"

"How am I supposed to know?"

"You aren't. Shit. Not only is it her, but her essence is going God knows where. How in the hell?"

There was a long silence as both tried to collect themselves enough to evaluate the situation. There was much punctually unspoken.

"What do we do?" Paul finally asked, almost in a whisper.

Tony didn't say anything for a few moments, and then replied affirmatively, "We don't tell anyone. And we find someone to protect her until it's her time."

"Tony, she's going to die!"

"Yes, and we have to make sure she does. It's about time we stop thinking that these things are up to us." Tony paused to think. When he was unsure, Susanna always found her way into his mind. His eyes went wide. "Remember, in '54 when I started looking for Susanna's essence?"

"You found it, no?"

"Yeah. Where's that kid now?"

CHAPTER 9

– Pay Attention –

September 1979, Kingston, New Jersey

Beck sat in a lecture hall at Princeton, in the fiftieth row of fifty rows in khakis and a grey t-shirt that used to be white. He slouched in a plastic chair that looked like it came straight out of a high school. He was decaffeinated and unshaven.

"All right, ladies, it's 6 a.m., let's get this going. There's coffee brewing, it'll be ready when we're done." A confident voice boomed from the front of the lecture hall. Two men in their fifties walked in, followed by armed police who stood at both doors. Beck had debated showing up, but now his attention was caught.

To Beck, the guy looked professional enough. He had a greying brown hippie beard, charisma, and purple-rimmed aviators tucked in his light blue dress shirt pocket. He looked as though he could be on the front of every major magazine in the country, whether it be for research or not. The other guy, fumbling through what looked like speech notes, was much paler, about the same age, and his formerly bright orange-and-blonde tufts were turning a sort of French-vanilla white. He reminded Beck of that scene in *Rudolph the Red-Nosed Reindeer* where the Santa puppet starts to get old and his orange hair shows streaks of white. Beck pressed his fingers into his eyes, and made slow circles, trying to relieve them of the exhausting and painful pressure behind his eye sockets from a string of sleepless nights. He wasn't so sure that sleep would help dull the vivid memories he'd been revisiting as of late. Beck opened his eyes and smiled. He was really comparing this highly touted professor to Santa Claus. He needed coffee. Nothing could jolt one into the consciousness of longing like the smell of brewing coffee, waiting for the pot to breathe its readiness with the promise of alertness.

Beck glanced around at the other people in the impressive lecture hall that looked somewhat like a massive log cabin. The wood looked like honey, or maple syrup, on top of peanut butter, smeared to a thick gleam on the chocolate-chip pancakes. His dad used to make them this way on Sundays, before Beck had to help shovel the snow walls at the end of the driveway. Now that he thought of it, he never really helped much with his miniature shovel. Binta sometimes came too, and Beck was struck again by how much he missed her, picturing the peanut butter and honey dripping off their noses. It had been four years. It had been four long and lonely years, rather, working in the library to save money for this day. Beck had enjoyed the quiet though. There was so much in the silence, closed off between the thousands of bindings that lined the shelves. The books depended so heavily on someone choosing to open them.

Beck's stomach backflipped. He looked around the room for another distraction, noticing that this not-quite-comfortable room was encased in a massive grey stucco building that looked like a cross between a dentist's office and a quarantine ward. Apparently, these were the most malleable young minds in the world, and here Beck was, sincerely missing his 8 a.m. physics lectures at Princeton, only a few minutes' drive away in his "burnt-to-shit-red pickup," as his aunt liked to say. This had to be what he wanted to do though. He loved research. He was very sure. He needed to do it. *This was supposedly where research got interesting, right? When you throw yourself in the deep end of it before it's understood?*

"Does anyone know what déjà vu is?" said the cooler of the two guys.

"A guardian angel, perhaps?" said the slightly less cool one, who Beck now knew had some semblance of an English accent, mixed with somewhere in New York.

"I'm Dr. Anthony Crypt."

"Dr. Paul Elliott." They both paused and shook one another's hands and the room laughed dully.

"Let's start with an easy one." Dr. Crypt winked. "What do you picture life being like after death? Anybody? Bit of a paradox, huh?"

The room was deathly silent, as if everyone was ready to literally find out in that exact moment. Dr. Crypt's pause felt longer than it was.

"Well." He raised his eyebrows, almost in a smirk as he turned around and laughed, putting his sunglasses on. He turned back around rapidly. "What if we, mostly I, told *you*, that we are able to send somebody into your mind during the year you are supposed to die, to access all of your memories?" The silence continued, but you could almost feel the many deep inhales going straight to the brain.

"We're looking for stories, and where minds, souls, and memories — essences if you will, are needed next. We ask: Who are they needed by?" Dr. Elliott replied, somewhat harshly. "Of course, the science of this endeavour is my end of the bargain, Tony does the media show."

"Don't get your feathers in a knot, Paul," Tony mocked in a British accent, paused and looked down, shoving his hands in his pockets the way he had for years, and paced across the stage that was smaller than his mind. "Is there a Becker Brooks here?" He mumbled the words so fast that Beck almost didn't catch his own name. Tony was looking directly at him before he even stood up. Beck didn't think he stood out either, everyone was wearing the same damn thing.

"Uh, yes, sir, doctor sir," Beck mumbled loudly as he stood up. He wasn't so cool and hidden now.

"Fantastic," Tony said sarcastically. "Room 233 at 8 p.m." Paul stared, stunned at Tony. This was not the time.

"Sir, why so late?" Beck replied.

"This is already a more public conversation than it should be, don't you think, Brooks?" Tony put "public conversation" in air quotations. Beck noticed the officers at the door turning to see the commotion. Beck sat back down, thinking he'd better shut up. Why the hell did Dr. Crypt need to see *him*? The sense of urgency he felt at twenty-five should have given him a heart attack. Beck wasn't unlike Tony Crypt and he was about to find that out faster than he wanted to.

"So." Dr. Crypt clapped his hands together loudly and shoved them back in his pockets. Beck watched as Paul shuffled over to the officers at the doorway, clearly ensuring that there was no trouble. Beck only then realized the glass of rum on the podium.

"You all work for the government now, like us. This is the most fundamental research that has happened for mankind and here you all are! Shit, you should all have some rum too, shouldn't you?" Tony was now, Beck realized, unquestionably drunk. Paul cut in bleakly.

"You will all be trained to sort through the next generation of memories. You're going to be the next Sifters."

#

After the long debrief earlier that day, Beck found himself walking up to a door that looked like it belonged on the water edges of Venice. It had that odd pyramid top and smelled, not badly, but of damp wood from the moisture of open-mouthed napping inside. It was a deep brown and was casually placed. It wouldn't be casual anywhere else in the dentist-office-white hallways. Beck put his fist up to knock, realizing the door was propped open ever so slightly. He poked his nose in.

"Um, Dr. Crypt?" He checked his watch after a few seconds of silence. 8:03 p.m.

"Dr. Cry...?"

"Brooks, come in." Tony was sitting with his elbows on his knees in an expensive pine-green recliner in the corner, facing away from both the window and his desk. His blaring alcohol collection was directly to his left, but Beck had already smelled it from the hall. Tony was rubbing sleep out of his eyes, which looked aged, pained, and an exhausted milky black. Now Beck pegged him around sixty.

"Uh, hi, sir, I'm Becker Broo..."

"Yep, I know, kid, have a seat. Scotch? No, you're a beer type, hm?"

"I, uh, I'd love one, sir." Tony reached behind him and pulled out an IPA, half stood up to hand it to Beck and shook his hand, adding "Tony" and smiling briefly.

"Sit, Brooks, please." Beck didn't realize he hadn't sat down yet. In this odd way he felt connected to the pain of Tony's exhaustion, but afraid of what he was about to tell him. Beck suddenly missed his father, and grabbed a small pen pendant around his neck, gently tugging the chain so that it came undone and lay gently in his palm. He put his elbows on his knees and flipped it over and over between his forefinger and thumb, as if waiting for it to give him a burst of confidence or sense of what to do next. His father had been a carpenter, but he wrote hypnotic poetry. The necklace had been a gift to Beck's father, from his mother.

The room was quiet besides the subtle hum of the radiator. Beck could feel Tony's gaze on him. Neither one of them knew who should continue the conversation. Tony saw himself in Beck and hesitated for a moment. Was this the right kid, or was he going to see himself in anyone who could do this job? It had to be Becker Brooks though. He knew that much. Tony hated that he felt wrong about it, but then again, he felt wrong about a lot these days.

"Sir?" Beck didn't raise his head for a few seconds after he spoke.

"Hm?"

"What am I doing here?"

"Well, how much time you got?" Tony smiled, trying to be welcoming, but becoming acutely aware of the harsh, burning smell of alcohol.

"Three beers?" Beck smiled shyly, hoping his joke wasn't too forward. "Of course, if that's okay, sir."

"I've got time for as many as we need, how about that?" Tony knew that what he was about to explain to this kid was beyond the scope of anything taught. It was even more erratic because Tony taught it to himself, and as Paul would say, that's the first problem. Tony needed Beck to trust him, and he felt unexpected guilt in that he couldn't tell Beck everything just yet. But he would have to make him think he did in order for this to work. Tony was nervous. He hadn't fully explained the science of what he and Paul were doing to anyone yet. Even Mark only knew the bare minimum and Tony planned on keeping it that way. Mark overestimated the price of their freedom. Tony was willing to lose it by not paying the rent.

"You know, we don't have to talk about things just yet. What's your situation? What's your mantra? What gets you out of bed in the morning?"

"Well, sir, I graduated about four years ago."

"Right, so sub in the crummy apartment now? You've been saving all this time, huh?"

"Yeah." Beck smiled at the floor. He paused for a moment. "I am trying to find myself, sir. I lost my folks when I was young. I've kind of been on my own since." Tony already knew the answer to most of these questions.

"I lost mine too, kid, so did Paul." Tony paused a moment on these words. He allowed himself to feel Beck's pain, watching his shoulders sink. "Where are you from, Brooks?"

"The area. Grew up in Chester, Jersey."

"Why are you here?"

"Um, well you asked me to come?"

"No, why are *you* here?"

Beck paused for a second, still confused by the question. Why *was* he here? Why had he agreed to do this in the first place? The Sifting Project wasn't public knowledge. It was a prestigious government research initiative like Area 51 or whatever other conspiracy theories or speculations were actually truthful enough to be hidden behind barbed wire fences for the next thirty years. He wasn't one for conspiracy theories — they complicate public trust, but now he was living one and it was different. Beck now knew people were recruited for the Sifting Project, like he was, but he didn't understand why. Beck thought of Binta.

"I want to help people, I suppose. I want things to be fair and right and just, and if I can do my part at all I'd like to."

"And you think working in a secret research sector that withholds information from people was the way to do that?"

"Well they are the utmost authority. I suppose they would be doing it with the world's best interest in mind?"

"Interesting." Tony paused and took a swig of his drink, standing up to lock the door and lean against it. He set his drink down and shoved his hands in his pockets. He looked up and made rigid eye contact with

Beck. "Let me tell you something. People might think they have the world's best interest in mind. But they don't stop to wonder if they are in any way misguided. The people at the top are the ones who are least likely to have anyone else's best interest in mind, not necessarily by their individual doing, but the system's. It's horrible, terrible, really. But it's a system designed to keep them where they are, and not let anyone else in. If the system is antiquated, even new people with more informed values filtering through it still uphold it regardless."

"But, sir, you work for them."

"Do I?"

"I don't understand."

"Well I do and I don't. Always been in limbo."

"Huh?"

"Listen, what I am about to offer you is a job that I need you, and only you to do, which you might have suspected by now. But if your morals lie entirely with authority then you should probably leave."

"They don't."

"Great. Because we're about to break every rule there is. We're not going to listen to a damn thing they have to say and pretend like we are. About twenty-five years ago, a doctor named Mark Jones was put in charge of the Sifting Project. Before, he was our supervisor when we worked for NASA. The Sifting Project utilizes the research Paul and I did at your age. I'll explain more about that later. The project was initially designed to keep specific memories and secrets internal, to protect America from another war. It's not that anymore, and we don't know how much oversight there is above Mark, or if it is just him. Regardless, we need to redirect the implications of these actions because things have gone detrimentally awry. I'm asking you to help me fix this. Make sense?"

"Understood." Beck was captivated and terrified at the same time. He actually wasn't sure he understood but he wanted Tony to think he did.

"Are you sure? You look a little pale?"

"I'm sure."

"All right, well, let's hit the nail on the head!"

"Yes, sir." Beck sat up straighter in his chair, which made Tony smile.

"You ever wonder what your memories do?" Tony felt an odd nostalgia. Twenty-five years prior, he sat with Paul trying to explain the same thing. This time he knew much more and was confident he was doing the right thing.

"They help us remember our lives, I guess?"

"Yes, but you see…" At that moment Paul unlocked and opened the door, peeking his head in.

"Am I interrupting?" he asked.

"Not at all," Tony replied sarcastically, glaring playfully at Paul. Beck remained silent. He was unsure of where his voice was welcome.

"This is Becker Brooks," Tony continued, motioning to Beck sitting timidly in the chair opposite him, beer in hand.

"Ah, it's a pleasure, Mr. Brooks, we've been looking for you for some time now." Paul reached out to shake Beck's hand. For such a thin man, Beck was surprised by the strength of his grip. "What have I missed?" Paul asked.

"Everything. I've explained it all. Too bad, you probably could have helped me too," Tony replied, winking at Beck.

"What a shame. Do catch me up."

Beck sat upward even further in his seat. This was it. He had no idea what he was in for, but he wanted to do what was right, and he felt that the only reason one goes behind the government's back is to make things right. It might not even be their doing. Who was this guy Mark Jones? Beck was startled by how much he trusted Tony. He hadn't read Paul enough yet but he and Tony seemed to be amicable. Only later would Beck realize how much he envied their friendship.

"We were just starting, so yes, you interrupted," Tony said.

"I'm sure we're even," Paul replied.

"Anyway, Beck, let's get another drink and get started, shall we?" Tony said, snapping Beck from his momentary thoughts.

"Yes, absolutely, sir."

"Oh you get sir, huh?" Paul replied to Beck's answer.

"Yes, and rightfully so," Tony said as he reached behind him and grabbed another beer for Beck. "How much do you know, kid?"

"Only what you said today in the presentation, sir."

"All right, so there may have been some white lies in there somewhere, but most of it was right. Let's start at the beginning. In 1950, Paul and I were beginning our post-college careers, much like you. At the time we were working for what would become NASA in 1958. You learned this today. Questionably legally, we were working on a project in an undisclosed location, because we were interested in what happens to us after death." Tony pretended to slit his throat and continued, "As we know, matter cannot be created or destroyed, so it makes no logical sense why something as powerful and prominent as the human mind would just disappear when you die. Its energy must go somewhere. So we started tracking people's infrared energy using really basic GPS and satellite technology which we had at the time."

"Isn't GPS only a few years old?" Beck asked.

"To you," Paul replied. He was still leaning against the door. Beck didn't notice he had closed and locked it again.

"We found something incredible. The energy from the human brain begins to climb in the last year of life, reaching its peak momentarily after death, and then gradually comes back down. The most fascinating, is that its energy level appears to be on a string with a new human being. In the last year of life, this energy, as we have researched, is a complex reconstruction of the mind, largely composed of memory clouds and webs — they look very much like neural synaptic connections, which are essentially brain cells firing between one another. It begins to separate from the physical brain in your last year of life. This is why people become unexpectedly reflective in their final year, whether they know their death is approaching or not. The essence of their life, if you will, composed of their memories, then begins to appear in an unborn child, or more clearly, around the stomach area of pregnant woman. The energy signatures are the exact same. We've done millions of trials, and this is the case in each one. Interestingly, though many essence energy signatures are extremely similar, no two people alive at once have the same one."

"Later," Paul picked up, "we found that through a sort of astral projection, we can access these essences and enter them, experiencing the memories of someone else as if we were there. The downside is that the clarity of the experience is based off of what the person remembers. We can only see what they have seen, and how they remember it."

"But that may not be reflective of reality, right? People's memories make mistakes," Beck replied. He was sitting so close to the edge of his seat he almost fell off. He took a long swig of his beer.

"Precisely," Paul replied, "but a memory is someone's truth. It is their story. That's what makes them valuable, especially, if by nature of being, they threaten the system meant to silence them. They speak for the truth."

"So, so, so, what do the Sifters do then?"

"Well here's where it gets even more interesting," Tony replied. "Memories and life experiences naturally determine where their essence goes when they die. Essences are organically crafted into a package of memories at the end of every person's life. They are most vulnerable and only accessible here. If you tamper with their memories, this changes the natural trajectory of the essence. If you know which memories to tamper with, you can direct the essence wherever you want, stop that person from dying, or kill them sooner. By changing the trajectory to someone the government has raps on, you're essentially silencing a story and a truth. The government didn't like the idea that knowledge was passed at a random they couldn't control. It's not hereditary or the mother would need to die."

"Why would anyone do that?"

"That's what the Sifters do."

"Why?"

"Those with power in this country believe that they can create desirable trajectories and promote a sort of non-hereditary monarchy. After the Second World War, throughout the Vietnam War, and now in the middle of the Cold War, they're afraid of the speed that intelligence can travel at. They're also afraid of their past, the events that they're responsible for and the tragedies and oppression that they've perpetuated. The Sifting Project was a way to silence and contain essences, essentially memories, and experiences, that could speak against them. If they can ensure that these essences are passed to someone favourable — someone with power, status, and certain experiences in society, then they can keep things contained. They think this tactic is their best chance against another war. There is perhaps some truth here with select essences. There are people who have been saved and eliminated, but the project has gone far beyond its initial intent — the scope of people being sifted now has grown exponentially, and at whose hand we're honestly not entirely sure. They've become detrimentally afraid of what they don't know, not unlike how much people fear death. A person's truth is threatening to those who created it and someone has done work to silence all potential threats. Paul and I are unfortunately very much accomplices. The thing we don't know yet, and haven't been able to figure out for decades, is how we access memories of a more distant past — the dormant essences within us. Once an essence is passed, we don't know how to access it. That's what the government's afraid of and why they're doing all this. They fear the day someone figures it out. We clearly don't think this is a process that just showed up twenty-five years ago. It's much bigger than we understand, and there is knowledge there along with the experiences of those who lived it, that everyone wants to control."

There was a long silence. Beck didn't know what to say. *Whose memories and experiences do I have, lying dormant in my mind? Where are they? Why are they there?*

"Why would you two agree to this?"

Tony looked at the floor, squinting his eyes together. "Because we were promised our freedom." For the first time, Tony truly felt ashamed.

Beck gulped. "I don't understand."

"We didn't have a choice. Our lives were threatened, among others."

"But, what about everyone else's life?"

"It's a glorified shit show, I know," Tony interrupted.

Paul nodded in agreement. "That's why you're here and that's why we're here now. To make it right."

"How?"

Tony and Paul made eye contact. Paul nodded. "There's much more we need to explain, but essentially, there's a girl, and we need you to sift through her memories," Tony replied.

"I'm confused. I'm not sifting anyone."

"You won't be in that sense, but we need you to go into her memories and protect her from the Sifters who will try to."

"Why is she so important?"

"Her essence's trajectory is headed…" Tony paused, taking a deep breath, "in three thousand different directions."

#

Beck had no idea what he was signing up for, but he did know he felt drawn to it. He trusted Tony in a way he couldn't describe, though it seemed that Tony trusted Paul in another odd sense. They all trusted each other in some symbiotic symphony, knowing they'd need to if they were going to orchestrate what they were wading into. A few strands of the same life were intertwining, bricked off from the rest of the world where they were free to weave, and do something with the braid. Beck sat in his car, gripping the steering wheel as the tires slid over the slushy September dirt on the damp roads. He was driving to Tony and Paul's house.

#

It was a cool Monday morning like all twenty-five years prior, and Tony and Paul were setting up the equipment they needed in their basement. They were banking on the fact that Mark would think they were using it to test data points. Besides, both Tony and Paul were waiting for Mark to crumble under old age anyway. Mark was old now, and knew nothing about the details of the Sifting Project compared to the polymath Tony believed himself to be, so they were confident in safe use despite their reputation of being untrustworthy.

"Are we really about to drag this poor kid into this, Tony?" Paul asked, fiddling with tangled wires.

"Yes, I like *this* kid."

"So do I and that's what I'm worried about."

"Why are you never worried about how *you* could affect the situation?"

"Because I am a constant variable. I have no idea what *you* are going to do." There was a long pause. "I think the last time we actually set this up was in the '50s when we built it. It's so old. The ones they use now must be better."

"Probably." Tony was fiddling with the cords of the machine. It really looked like something Superman was shipped to Earth in, but it was the only way they could ensure safe astral projection to allow Beck to sift. Tony had given Beck the address on Friday when they met in his office at the school and said to be here at 9 a.m. sharp. It was 8:57 and Tony was a bit antsy. He might have been a rough-and-tumble kind of doctor, but he was punctual. He knew college kids thought 9 a.m. meant knocking on the door at 9 a.m. He had thought that way once too. But a small part of him worried the kid wouldn't show. He re-evaluated, and felt he knew that Beck wouldn't be the type to be late.

"Paul, would you go upstairs and wait in the kitchen for the kid?"

"The door is unlocked."

"He's not going to just walk into our house."

"Fine." Paul rolled his eyes and headed upstairs. He sat down at the kitchen table and stirred his oatmeal that had been too hot to eat earlier. Now it was too cold. He heard a soft, timid knock on the door. He stood, and could see a tall and thin boy through the glass slits between the emerald curtains on either side of the door. Tony had insisted that they not be the same claustrophobic opaque ones in the kitchen, and thus they were translucent and brightened the foyer with a shimmer of green light. It was still warm for September, but damp. Beck was wearing a NASA t-shirt and ripped jeans. He reminded Paul too much of Tony, and he paused for a moment before opening the door.

"Hey, Brooks." He moved aside to make way for Beck to enter. "How are you this morning? You have trouble finding the house?"

"I'm good, and no, it's the only one for miles though. Why so isolated?" Beck stepped in the house, bending down to take off his sneakers.

"Oh no need, it's a bit of a mess downstairs anyway. What did you ask, sorry?"

"Oh, okay, um, why so isolated?"

"Well I suppose it'd be difficult to be living in a big city and do what we're doing downstairs. It's worked out for what we're going to ask of you."

"Right." Beck looked at the floor, shoving his hands in his pockets.

"We're nervous too," Paul reassured.

"How are people going to know that anything has changed? Nobody would really know any different, right?"

"I'm assuming with the turn of events, a lot of things will be unearthed," Paul replied.

"Hm." Beck gulped and shoved his hands deeper into his pockets. Paul noticed this too.

"Would you like something to drink? Did you eat breakfast? Probably not, I'm guessing?"

"Shouldn't we get to work?"

"Ah, Tony is tinkering down there setting things up. He could be a while. Besides, I haven't really had a chance to talk with you yet." Paul placed a hand on Beck's shoulder, guiding him to the kitchen. He had a feeling Beck was a little skeptical of him.

"I'd love some orange juice."

"Sure thing. We have quite a lot of jam as well," Paul replied, half laughing. "Tony really likes raspberries." Paul rolled his eyes and Beck laughed. He was surprised by how human and relatable these two incredible doctors were.

"Sure, I'd love some on toast." Beck smiled.

Paul picked out a piece of toast on the counter. The loaf was freshly made by the same lady who made the jams. She lived a few miles up the road and was surely in love with Tony. Tony, of course, took full advantage of this and had her baking them a loaf of pumpernickel and jarring a few raspberry jams each week.

"You like your toast dark? Light? Medium?"

"Dark, please."

"You got it. Please, sit." Paul motioned to Tony's seat at the table behind him. Beck sat and looked out the window at the beautiful rolling hills of green, periwinkle forget-me-nots, daisies, and dandelions. He wondered if this is where Tony sat in the morning and how idiosyncratic it felt that he drank normal things like orange juice and ate toast with raspberry jam. Given the gravity of the situation, the pair were dusted in a calmness and normalcy that Beck had yet to feel for himself. He noticed a smoke tree outside the window, the leaves a bruised dark purple, as if from decades of the velocity of open-field wind. The house was intoxicatingly un-pious.

It smelled strongly of leather and peppermint, which both Tony and Paul must have become nose-blind to by now.

The toast popped out of the toaster and Beck snapped from his thoughts. Paul placed the jam, a spoon, a glass of orange juice, and the toast on an emerald green plate in front of him. Beck smiled. The spoon must be a British thing. Or maybe just a Tony and Paul thing. Paul sat down across from him.

"What's on your mind, Mr. Becker Brooks?"

"A lot of things, sir. I don't really know where I fit here, you know?"

"I do. I still wonder the same thing at fifty-three." Paul laughed. "Talk to me."

Beck took a swig of his orange juice, which tasted fresh. "Did you make this?"

"Goodness, no, this little old lady who has taken a liking to Tony makes it. She makes the bread and jam too. She lives up the street. You might have passed her farm on the way in. If you stop by on the way home and say you know us, I'm sure she'll get you a fresh supply." Paul winked.

"I will." Beck smiled and downed the rest of his juice.

"All right, now answer the question." The comfort Paul gave felt forced. There was something lying dormant behind Paul's eyes, but Beck was unsure of who it was waiting for.

"Well, my folks died when I was a little kid and all I've really got are my cousins who are in high school and college now, and my aunt Mary who raised me. My best friend died from cancer. She was kind of like a big sister. Her husband and kids live in California. She was my babysitter before my parents died. I suppose I took a liking to astrophysics after the moon landings and NASA, and I went into that in my undergrad like everyone else and then was randomly recruited for this. I didn't even graduate summa. I feel like I've just coasted blankly through everything."

"Because you're lonely?"

"Well, yes. And confused."

"About?"

"I guess I'd like to know how Sifters are chosen." Beck had been wary of the fact that many of the people in the lecture hall the other day were much older than he was, and he had a terrible feeling.

Paul tried not to show his disappointment in Beck's question. He wasn't a good liar.

"They're chosen by the government, usually people who don't have much and would dedicate their time to the task. People who are unusually bright," Tony answered, standing in the doorway with his sleeves rolled up and his forearms covered in smears of grease. He'd told as much of the truth as he could. The only way that sifting could work, was if the Sifter was also in their last year of life. Tony couldn't bring himself to tell Beck that yet. "You're sitting in my seat, Mr. Brooks."

"I told him to," Paul answered playfully.

"And that warrants what, exactly?" Tony answered. Neither Paul or Beck could tell if he was serious. Beck stood up.

"I didn't say you had to stand. Finish your toast." Tony winked at him. Beck smiled and sat back down, taking a bite. He still wanted answers.

"But why me?"

"Well I figured I'd come upstairs so we could talk about that." He walked over and sat in the chair to Beck's right. Beck watched him, and made eye contact to show that he was listening.

"So, here's the thing. Her name's Penny." Tony pushed passed her name so nonchalantly, as if it didn't matter. Beck felt that there was more here. He tried to just listen first, before he asked too many questions.

"Okay."

"Okay, here's a photo of her, so you know who you're looking for." Tony slid a black-and-white photograph across the table. The girl was wearing a dark turtleneck and a plaid skirt. She was sitting comfortably on what looked like a park bench, her hands folded in her lap. The black spindly trees behind her arched into the sky like a mirror of her wavy dark hair, as if calling the clouds to expedite spring and bring them life. Even in the photograph Beck could tell that her eyes were either green or blue by their lightness.

"She's beautiful," Beck said.

"Yes, she is," both Tony and Paul replied. Tony pulled the photograph back, which Beck now noticed was dated ten years prior. *How long had Tony and Paul known about this girl?*

"Let's talk rules, because there are definitely a few of them. You want a coffee? More OJ? More toast would do you some good."

Beck's nerves had overthrown his appetite. "A coffee would be great, thanks." He sat stunned, staring at the photo. There were a few fault lines in his reverence for the two doctors. There was something they weren't telling him.

"Paul, would you?"

"Of course," Paul added sarcastically. "Anything else for his highness?"

"Shut up. I'm explaining important things."

"Well, I could also explain said important things."

"Right." Tony rolled his eyes and smiled at Beck, mouthing "No, he couldn't."

There was something reassuring about their bickering. Their hunger to agitate the other was a welcoming calm before the storm. Beck looked back at the smoke tree, wondering all it had seen and heard over the years.

"I still don't understand, sir. Why me?"

#

"All right, here we are." Tony had led the way downstairs while Paul cleaned up some of the dishes in the kitchen. "Sorry about the mess."

Beck's eyes darted around at the mounds of wires, and old technology askew in absolutely every corner. He figured Tony was down here much more often than Paul was.

"We're going to take this slow," Tony reassured Beck, whose eyes were wide and darting around the room, coming to a stop on a machine. There was a piece of tape above it on the wall which read: "APM" in thick marker. Tony noticed Beck's hands in his pockets and smiled. "Okay, have a seat for me over there." He motioned to the two wooden stools under the black-board in the corner.

"What does APM stand for?"

"We'll get to that. Sit," Tony said a little more sternly.

"Okay, okay."

"We're stuck with this cruddy office, which to be honest, is fine. I'll take a basement in my house versus a basement janitor's office."

"You worked in a janitor's office?" Beck asked, surprised.

"Yes," Tony sighed, "momentarily. It wasn't our best moment, but then again neither was the past two decades. All right, rules."

Beck's face grew up all at once, searching Tony's eyes, which still took him aback. The cross-hatching of pain and dismembered thought in them struck him.

"Number one, you never turn this thing off. Ever." Tony handed Beck the most sophisticated watch he'd ever seen, which Beck took and put on.

"What is..."

"It's a tracker. It makes sure you know what day and time it is for your physical body, and what day and time your astral body is in, in Penny's memories. On it, you can scroll through Penny's memory timeline and select a point to go to. This will send a signal to me, to send your astral body to that point. So of course you can't screw around because I approve of all your hopping about."

Beck was lost. Tony was going much too quickly. "I'm..."

"Confused, I know. It's fine. Kind of has to be trial and error. We're going to do a test run."

"Am I supposed to get into that thing?" Beck's voice was shaking slightly. He motioned to the APM in the corner, hooked up to hundreds of different-coloured wires.

"Oh, that mess?" Tony looked at it and paused for an uncomfortably long time. "Absolutely!"

"Reassuring."

"Because it's old? It's the first one we made but it works *great*. Like old movie stars! They may not look as hot but they can still act!"

"Shit," Beck mumbled under his breath.

"Hm?"

"Nothing. Could you go over the rules again?"

"Good save. You. Are going to get in there." Tony pointed to the APM. "APM stands for Astral Projection Machine which sounds tacky so we say APM to make it at least sound like a cool acronym."

"Okay, so you're going to separate my physical and astral body? How does that even work for sifting?"

"Depending on what you believe, humans are a sort of multidimensional being. It turns out your astral body is made up of the same types of things that the essences are, though they are different." Tony spoke quickly. He couldn't be entirely truthful, which he hoped Beck wouldn't catch on to. "They are pretty much the same damn thing, actually, which is why you can get into Penny's essence."

"Right." Beck's stomach pulled in and out like the tides. He could taste the acid from the jam and orange juice in his arid throat.

"So, I'm going to put you under and choose a date for you. Just a few hours ago should be good. You're going to go find Penny *without* being seen."

"Well that's nerve-wracking."

"Eventually it won't be an issue."

"Wait, why? I'm going meet her?"

Tony sighed deeply. "Yes, you are. We discussed this. Right?"

"Abstractly, sir."

"You are going to meet her, but don't worry about that yet. Right now is just a test run so you know what it feels like. Put this in your ear."

"What does *this* do?"

"It lets you talk to me. Don't turn it off either." There was a long pause before Beck asked, "Why are you doing this? You asked me so I think it's fair that I ask you."

"My conscience, maybe my morals?" Tony replied with partial truth.

"I don't believe you, sir."

"Ah, well. That's tough isn't it?"

Beck climbed into the machine, and laid down on the gel mat, which was pre-molded for a body. It wasn't the most uncomfortable. The APM had walls as thick as a pumpkin when you're trying to carve it. For a moment he felt claustrophobic which he never had before. The machine door was opened to his left and would close over his whole body. It was a sort of dull beige, and had coloured wires running all along and pegged to the insides of the walls. Some of the wires hung from the sides with what looked like stethoscope endings on them. Tony clicked a few buttons and reached in, grabbing these loose wires. He paused on Beck, holding his gaze. He took a deep breath.

"I believe there are many people out there, like me, who would agree that the Sifting Project is complicatedly wrong if they knew about it, but they will choose to do nothing. They will choose not to see it unless it affects them. For the entirety of my life I did exactly that — nothing. I was apathetic toward something that I knew was wrong. I ignored the potential for truth in the stories of the past, present, and future. I suppose now I'm choosing to listen."

"Listen to what?"

"Them. People. The public really only remembers what has been recorded. It's always been that way. But there are records of unedited stories and accumulated insight out there that have been destroyed or silenced because of me. Before we tampered with them, they were passed between generations through essences. There may be a perfect plan in place to pass them along, and one day, unlock them to correct this mess we've made. It's a plan we don't understand. We shouldn't have fucked with it but we have. Now I'm trying to fix it. And Penny is how."

"Why Penny, do you think?" Beck's eyes were wide. He hadn't expected the seriousness to come spewing out of Tony.

"She has a knack for making good memories. You'll see. She's chosen to listen her whole life."

"And me?" Beck was impatient with this question now. Tony had avoided it each time, though with impressive skill.

"Shirt up, please."

Beck lifted up his t-shirt and Tony suctioned the tips of the wires to his chest.

"This is just so I know you aren't dead."

"Why me?" Beck asked assertively, grabbing Tony's wrists.

Tony froze. He was startled by Beck's strength.

"It could have been anyone and you chose me," Beck said sternly.

"I didn't."

"What does that mean?"

"I didn't choose you. Something did. All I did was figure that out. Your essences have very similar compositions."

"What does that mean? Do Sifters and Siftees need to have similar essences for this to work?"

"I don't know," Tony replied. Beck was annoyed. He wasn't sure if he was stupid or if Tony was purposely withholding information from him. He also felt afraid of failing to fill duty's shoes. He felt inescapably heavy.

"Sometimes the clothes are too big, kid. But we have to wear them anyway."

"Ah, I'm just in time, I see." Paul had come down the stairs, his shirt stained with water splashes.

"Yes," Tony replied nodding to Beck. "About to put him under."

Paul walked over to the APM, put his hand on Beck's shoulder, and smiled. "There will be plenty of toast and orange juice when you get back."

"Good to know," Beck answered nervously.

"All right, are you ready? Say yes." Tony leaned over the APM and grabbed the lid. Paul stepped back out of sight.

"Do I have a choice?" Beck uttered with a shaky sarcasm.

"You just listen to my voice when you wake up. It's going to feel and look a little weird, but I'll talk you through it once you're in. Just relax as best you can." Tony closed the lid.

"Wait, do you smoke?" Tony yelled through the glass.

"What? No!"

"Just checking. Nicotine can give horrible nightmares afterwards."

#

Paul waited until Beck was under. They had a few moments until he would gain consciousness.

"When are you going to tell him?" Paul asked coldly. Tony knew the question was coming, the pit had been rolling around in his stomach, collecting fear dust all morning.

"When I absolutely have to." Tony sighed.

"You care about him. He's a lot like you too, you know."

"And that's why I can't tell him yet."

"Tony, you can't hide from everyone you care about." Paul's tone became antagonistic.

"I'm not. I'm hiding *everything* from everyone I care about."

The most crucial piece of what would make their plan work, is what Tony could not bring himself to tell Beck. The astral projection explanation he had given was only partially true. It was a way to cover up the fact that all the APM was doing was tugging and stretching the connection between Beck's physical body and his partially pre-separated essence. Sifters are recruited because they can sift. They can sift because they, like their Siftees, are in their final year of life. Thus, their essence has begun to separate. Through a series of chemical reactions, the astral body, which many don't believe in, actually transitions into an essence. Essences can connect with and mingle with other essences through a complicated chemical process that Tony and Paul only understood on the surface. This was the crux of Tony and Paul's research. Why essences are only available from people who are nearing their expiration, was something that still puzzled Tony and Paul, along with who natural essence trajectories are determined by.

Tony hadn't dared to look where Beck's own essence was headed. Usually, if you were recruited to be a Sifter, it didn't matter, but Tony realized now that this was precisely what he was fighting against. It should matter for everyone. It did ease his thoughts knowing that Beck's trajectory likely wouldn't be tampered with. Beck wasn't anyone important yet, but Tony was worried about something else. A Sifter was usually released from their duty a few months prior to their expiration, in the event that the connection between their essence and physical body stops being able to be reeled back in post-sifting. The connection grows weaker closer to death as separation occurs, and it becomes harder to return to your physical body from sifting. Beck was going to have to sift right up to the end. Tony didn't want to lose him any sooner than he had to, but he also feared that this plan wouldn't work. That's why it was essential that the connection between Penny and Beck was strong. The similarity of their essences would cause less tension for Beck's — the chemical reaction wouldn't be as demanding. Penny would keep him alive long enough for this to work.

"I'd love to hear what you think your part in this is, doctor," Tony asked coldly.

"I'm just living in the shadow of what you're doing. Didn't think my perception mattered. As long as we have jam and bread, right?"

"It's not just my bread to break." There was a tinge of confusion in Tony's voice.

"I need empathy, not sympathy, Tony." Paul turned and walked up the stairs, leaving Tony standing somewhat startled, with his hands in his pockets, staring at Beck asleep in the APM. Tony sat down at a monitor connected to the APM and satellite technology that they had on the roof. It was what allowed him to stretch and shorten the distance between Beck's essence and his body. He punched in the coordinates for Penny's essence and turned a dial to give Beck's enough energy to stretch and make the contact. Tony still marvelled that all of this occurred in the troposphere, so small that nobody could see it. All he had was a monitor telling him that the energy level in the room was dropping.

"I'm sorry, kid," he managed to mutter, seconds before he heard the first semblance of sound on his earpiece.

"Brooks? You with me yet?" Tony asked.

#

Beck felt an electrified pain in his skull as if he were colliding with a needle bed. He felt thick vibrational waves passing through his entire body. The nausea and disorientation dismembered his thoughts. The reach for consciousness from this tearing was like trying to bring two magnets of the same polarity together. His eyes were open but what he saw around him was a swirling of colours like a child's watercolour painting. His vision was narrowed, and he felt as though he could only see through the pupil of his eye. It was a narrow column of messy blues, greens, and browns. Momentarily, he blacked out from the shock.

When he woke, he found himself sitting on a poorly paved path lined with two rows of forest, leading to a road. A few two-storey apartment buildings sulked along the road, painted a dull and peeling mint green, accented with white shutters. They appeared to be made of stucco, which he noticed right away because it was something Aunt Mary absolutely could not stand. She was the type to buy a house made of it because she liked the interior and have it re-bricked. The other houses on the street were 1920's brick homes. To the far right, Beck could see train tracks.

Other than these noticeable landmarks, the world he was looking at felt isolated and not fully formed. Some things were crystal clear, like the clouds. Their dark, grey-blue shells, filled with due rain, curled in on the fluffy white insides like white water crashing violently into the beach. The colour contrast pulled out the green in everything beneath them. Some things, in comparison, were mere outlines, like a simple graphite sketch. Other things were an odd mix of both. Beck blinked and rubbed his eyes, expecting it to all be because he wasn't fully awake yet, but the clarity of each section of this view held. He remembered his earpiece.

"Tony?" he mumbled groggily.

"Ah, there's my guy," he heard Tony reply on the other end. His voice echoed and felt far away. He thought he sensed a small bit of concern.

"What, where, uh…" Beck tried to formulate some semblance of an intelligent question to ask.

"Patience. Yes, I have some explaining to do. You're in the south end of Princeton. Actually, maybe just outside city limits."

"Why is everything so weird?"

"What do you mean weird?"

"It looks funny. Some things are clear, some aren't."

"Ah, yes," Tony replied. "You're in Penny's memories within her essence. You're seeing things as she remembers them. Of course, some things we pay more attention to, and remember more details of."

Beck was impressed. He was seeing someone's selective seeing. "So this is the epitome of understanding someone."

"Yes, in a way. What are you seeing?"

"Looks like a street, a few rundown apartments, and a train track?"

Tony was nervous. "Yes. Great. Penny is in the bottom apartment of the middle building. You see it?" Beck realized he was sitting in the middle of this path, his legs out in front of him and his arms and hands behind his back on the cement, holding him up. He stood immediately.

"Yes."

"Great. We're going to head there in a minute. I've got some more things to explain first."

Beck looked down at himself and held out his hands, looking at the pristinely clear details of his body. He was puzzled.

"Sir, I have a question?"

"Shoot."

"If these are Penny's memories, why am I so clear?"

Tony froze for a second, trying to conjure up an answer. Truthfully, it was because Beck's own essence, constructed of his own memories, was mingling with Penny's. In this sense, a reality of both of their memories is constructed. Beck had never been to this location before, and had no memory of it, so he was only seeing through Penny's memories. As for his own appearance, it was his own memory.

"She must have a memory of you. I don't know."

"But I'm so clear. How would she have seen me?"

"I'm not sure. Maybe she thought you were a hotshot. Like I said, this is selective visual input."

Beck accepted this, mostly because he liked the idea that she might have thought of him a few times. He had a fleeting doubt that there was a chance she could have remembered this much. Tony cut off Beck's train of thought intentionally, before he could ask further questions that Tony couldn't answer.

"All right, here's the last bit for now. Do you know why we only went a little ways back in time?"

"Because I have no idea what I'm doing?"

"Well you could screw up, yes. Chances are you will."

"Reassuring."

"Valid point but not why. The only sifting rule we will follow is this: you must sift chronologically, but backwards."

Beck thought about this for a second before beginning to ask why, but Tony cut him off.

"The reason is that this way, your presence won't affect future events."

"How?"

Tony sighed, which worried Beck a little. He wanted to seem competent.

"If you were to do the opposite, and begin when Penny was a child," Tony paused, gulping back any chance of emotion, "you'd change and affect her memories of the future by being present in her ones of the past. That could potentially alter the real future. By sifting backwards, you have no chance of doing that."

"I'm confused."

"If you introduce yourself to her now, her five-year-old self won't remember you from now. But the opposite would be true. If you introduce yourself to her five-year-old self, her thirty-one-year-old self will remember it. Make sense? That's a tough example but it will become more important as you show up throughout her life."

Beck understood and thought about this for a moment. "Am I going to have to reintroduce myself each time?"

"Precisely."

"That sucks."

"This isn't about getting the girl, Mr. Brooks. I didn't tell you it'd be fun, I told you it's important. Actually, quite imperative."

"Okay, I understand. What am I doing here again?"

"Really?" Tony sounded surprised so Beck thought it best to rephrase his question.

"I mean, what do you need me to do? Right now?"

"You had me worried there for a second, Brooks."

"I'm not that dense, sir."

"I want you to walk up to her apartment, and look in the window and see if you can see her."

"What? That's creepy! No way!"

"Not about getting the girl, remember?"

"Doesn't matter!"

"Keep your voice down! Walk up and see if you can see inside. Please?" Beck rolled his eyes and looked over at the apartment.

"There's a guy in a black suit knocking on her door."

"What?" Tony asked insistently. He could feel his heart rate rising.

"Yeah. I can't see his face. It looks like she's looking out the window to see him. Who is he?"

"Someone who isn't supposed to be there, likely. Might be a government-sanctioned Sifter. It's okay, this isn't an important memory."

"How do you know what's an important memory?"

"They're the ones most strongly dictating the essence's trajectory. Often major life events, but not always. I'll show you when you get back."

"What should I do?"

"Wait until whatever is going to happen, happens. It's not supposed to happen. Can you see her?"

"Yes, she's talking to the man."

"What does she look like?" Tony asked, trying desperately to hide his nervousness.

"She, um, her hair is long and dark and wavy. She's tall. Wearing baggy jeans and a faded red ABBA t-shirt. She's holding a notebook and a pen, I think."

Tony smiled, a single tear creeping its way down the crevices of the lines in his face. *Thank you, God*, he thought.

CHAPTER 10

– Validate –

October 1979, Kingston, New Jersey

Tony and Paul were sitting at their kitchen table on a Monday evening in the beginning of October of 1979. They were waiting for Beck's car to pull up at the front door. Tony was tapping his foot rapidly under the table and avoiding his breakfast. Paul thought he looked even thinner than usual. Tony didn't seem to hear the comment, as he didn't seem to hear most things other than his own thoughts.

Tony was anxious to get to work. He was always anxious when he wasn't working but today carried a little more weight. Beck was finally going to meet Penny after a month of practising going in and out of her memories, switching dates and times and keeping a low profile. Beck was going to an important memory today and Tony was nervous about hearing Penny's voice again. An important memory also meant that there could be Sifters around, and he hoped Beck was prepared. Tony had told Paul he was monitoring Penny's trajectory for changes, though he spent hours simply watching her memories, swimming in regret.

Tony and Paul were still only partially sure about which of Penny's memories were vulnerable. Because they didn't understand where her essence was going, they didn't know how to break down the web of memories within it. The only thing they had to go on was the fact that, in the web, some connections were more securely linked to the overall trajectory, which then splayed out into three thousand, nearly identical threads. As far as they could tell, these specific connections carried more weight in her life — they were the memories which made Penny who she was. These were also the types of memories that the Sifters typically sought to silence — they held truth, meaning, and pushed back against something that the government wished to keep quiet.

There were a few memories which formed a direct link with the lineage of Penny's essence. Other memories either connected loosely or were just spindles of her overall memory collection web. Things became dangerous when the stronger links were broken or tampered with.

Tony was banking on the fact that Penny's connections were stronger than any he had ever seen. But there was another aspect of this that puzzled him beyond any of the work he'd done before. It had nearly driven Tony mad over the past few days. In the live feed of Penny's essence, there were important connections that were her own memories — these were the ones that Beck was tapping in to. There were also others. They didn't light up on the screen like Penny's did, but they seemed to be diverging from a once converged point. They were almost dormant, as if they had been stored until now. They wrapped around Penny's own important memories like a vine, not to kill, but to cling to life in the path forward. Tony and Paul had noticed this in each of the essences they had worked with, logically wondering if these were essences of the past, waiting to be unlocked. They could never figure out how to do it, or where to find them. Penny's mind, uniquely, was flooded with these threads, and Tony couldn't help wondering if she knew they were there somehow. Whose stories did she have inside of her? This is truly what stirred Tony's mind. He wondered if the universe, or God, or something was trying to correct things, through her. She'd made him believe.

As Tony sat perplexed on his knees, watching these threads dance and gather across the screen, he thought of the voices, stories, and lives in the essences that he and Paul had helped silence, by cutting off their natural course. It now appeared that they might have been more persistent than Tony and Paul thought. Tony wanted to believe that they were still here, fighting to be heard through Penny. He put his head in his hands, moved and consumed by the thought that he could make things right. He was worried, as he watched slight changes occur on the screen. They were running out of time. He may never know how to unlock what was in Penny, and what she would pass on, but he could do the next right thing.

There was a loud knock on the door. Tony could hear Beck banging his boots against the mat outside to clean off the snow.

"Sometimes I wish he would just come in with his boots on and jump on the couch like a normal kid." Tony smiled at Paul, who was standing up to go let Beck in.

"He's not really a kid, you know."

"To us he is."

Paul knew Tony wasn't talking about missing his own teenage and young adult years. He was letting Beck's temporary presence in his life fill a void — fatherhood. Paul occasionally pitied Tony. He was too attached to yet another person he was bound to lose because of his job. Paul didn't often feel the same way as Tony did about most things, and when he did, he shoved it under heavier books. Paul never wanted a child, or a marriage or really anything that he could lose, though his heart had been opened. He wanted to go through the motions. Tony's presence was an added bonus, and Paul cared about him deeply which angered him. The one thing he couldn't lose, he hadn't yet. He distanced himself from worry when Tony's health slipped on a regular basis, though it terrified him. Tony had hurt and betrayed him, even if it was based in love. Though it might have been, Paul never considered his anger to be jealousy or envy. Tony had been distant too, until Beck. Despite the porcupine dilemma between them, Tony and Paul were connected in a passion and path that neither understood, but still followed, often unconsciously.

Paul opened the door for Beck. He came tumbling in rambling about his father's old car that Aunt Mary once drove, but now he drove, and how the only thing that *really* worked was the radio. All this fell out while he hung his coat up, took his boots off, pulled out his notebook and pen, and sat down at the kitchen table. Tony just grinned and had already stood and moved out of his usual seat so that Beck could sit in it. It was an uncharacteristic move on Tony's part. Tony sat with his chin resting on his hand, his elbow on the table. He looked content watching and listening to Beck, who finally sat down and noticed Tony's expression.

"What?"

"Oh nothing, just good to see you," Tony replied, trying to hide his smile.

"Oh, you too," Beck smiled, "and you, Paul."

"Always a pleasure, Beck," Paul replied. Paul looked at Tony and asked, "He seems pretty comfortable here anyhow?"

"Huh?" Beck replied.

"You're right," Tony answered Paul sarcastically.

"I'm always right."

"I'm confused," Beck replied.

"Which is fine," both Paul and Tony answered at the same time. There was a slight awkward silence before Paul asked Beck if he was hungry at all.

"I'm always hungry." Beck laughed.

"Oh we know," Paul answered. "What would you like?"

"Is there leftover ham?"

"Absolutely. Grilled cheese? Tomato soup?"

"Yes, please."

There was a warmth in the room that none of them had sensed before. Beck had grown to love the house, now coming as often as he could. Sometimes he forgot what he came for. It was distantly familiar to the three of them, and unfortunately brief.

"We've got important things to talk about while you get your stomach worked out. Are you able to stay the night tonight? We've got extra clothes and such when you get back from your task," Tony cut in. His tone was deliberate.

Beck gulped, stuttering fearfully over his words. What did this mean? "Yeah, I suppose."

"Great. Wasn't really a question."

Beck smiled. He was no longer intimidated by Tony's assertiveness, which once held his tongue. He saw the complicated relationship between Tony's humour and display of affection, or lack thereof. The more time he spent with Tony the more he felt he had grown into himself, and the more he felt at home. Rest was something Tony and Beck found in one another when they couldn't sleep. Beck loved his aunt and his cousins, though he had never connected with them like he did with Tony and Paul. Echoes of memories and experiences flowed between them, repeating pathways to achieve what uncoincidentally burned in their hearts.

#

Tony had mapped out Penny's entire memory timeline to date on the blackboard, not that Beck could understand any of his handwriting. Beck could tell this was an important day based on Tony's worried demeanour.

"So you're going back a little further today, Mr. Brooks. You're also going to meet her."

"So I can't screw up, is what you're telling me?"

"Exactly." Tony smiled nervously at Beck. "Here's the deal. You're going back three years. Once you do this, she'll also have suspicions in present day so we won't have much time."

"The furthest I've been back is six months!" Beck's voice crept higher as he spoke in mumbles of worry.

"Listen, any fight that happens from here on out is going to happen in present day and we will worry about that when the time comes. She doesn't know you in 1976, which is one of her first crucial memories. I'm going to give you free rein, as long as you stay within the boundaries we talked about. Don't go any further back than the date I give you. Anything past that date is fine. Do whatever you need to get her to trust you and to protect her. The hard part is the government Sifters. They try to blend in, but will be people she won't know. You just need to be aware, all the time. Oh and get a gun when you get there. You might need it."

"I do not know how to fire a gun!"

"Well it's not that hard, you'll get it."

"And what if I don't?"

"Just don't hit yourself."

"Funny."

"Beck, you'll be fine. You'll have me in comms if you need. Please don't turn it off."

"You're going to hear everything?"

"Yes."

"Why?"

"Because I know more than you."

"That's not a reason."

"I need to make sure you're doing the right thing."

"What's the wrong thing?" Beck was pushing Tony's buttons deliberately now. He was also genuinely curious. Tony seemed oddly protective of Penny.

"Just get in." Tony motioned to the APM.

Beck climbed into the machine and lay down, as usual, waiting for Tony to close the lid.

"All right, here's your deal: October 15th, 1976."

"How do you know what dates are important? From that thing?" Beck motioned to the monitor tracking the catalogue of essences.

"No, that tracks your essence's location. The one beside it zooms into and maps individual essence clouds. It's a live feed of the memory connections. The important ones form a direct link with the lineage and trajectory of an essence. Others float around and aren't as strongly linked. Disrupting the important ones, as you can imagine, changes the trajectory."

Beck sat up and looked over. It looked like a splayed rope on the screen — a rope of the energy of memories. Some wound more tightly to the general direction of the rope than others.

"And mine intertwines with hers when I sift?"

"Precisely." Tony felt the weight of worry. "You just need to ensure that her essence goes where it is meant to go, even if we have no idea why. Understand? I'm going to be monitoring the strength of the connections of her memories to the trajectory to make sure they don't weaken, or worse, disappear. That's basically your job. Don't give me more grey hair."

"All right. What about the man in the black suit? He keeps showing up?"

"I don't know who it is, but I'm working on it."

"So? Avoid him? And anyone else who looks like that?"

"Duh." Tony tried to smile. Earlier in the day they'd talked about Penny being dangerous, because love could be something that could easily alter memories. Tony had a bad feeling about this. Beck had Susanna's essence. That couldn't be a coincidence. He second-guessed nearly everything in his life, but he hadn't second-guessed Becker Brooks. "Just don't do any-thing I wouldn't do."

"Which leaves me nothing to work with."

Tony rolled his eyes and closed the lid of the APM. Beck couldn't hear him, but he mouthed "good luck." Beck was nervous, but also excited. He felt like he was needed and like he was doing something valuable. He hoped his parents could see him, as he fell into the dark dizzy spell of separation that initiated his connection with Penny's essence. Tony had said to him earlier, "You're a Sifter now, Brooks. But one with a moral compass. You're *the* Sifter. The others are just sheep."

#

When Beck began to gain consciousness again, he woke up in the same place he had the past few times he'd sifted. He was outside a small, local coffee shop on the main street of Sandy Hook, New Jersey, where Penny lived. She was a writer, which was all Beck knew about her. Tony had chosen not to share much of anything else. Beck liked the area because he could see it clearly. Penny knew it well, and spent a lot of time here, making it a convenient spot. Beck could easily navigate, because Penny had very clear memories of the surroundings. Once Beck came to his senses, he stood. He had learned that he couldn't interact with most of the people, because they were simply constructions of Penny's thoughts and memories. Unless it was someone she was interacting with, or had paid attention to as they passed, Beck didn't need to worry about being seen or being out of place. What he did need to worry about was how he was going to explain his presence to Penny.

"Brooks, are you awake yet?" Tony's voice startled Beck from his thoughts.

"Yes, I'm about to go in. Do you want my mic on?"

"No. I trust you with this one. Just keep her occupied for a few hours." Tony turned to the monitor and looked at the web of energy signatures on the screen. He thought they were beautiful. It was the closest he'd been to Penny since 1954. "Check back in when you're done, not before about 6 p.m. where you are. Got it?"

"Easy." Beck was looking through the window of the coffee shop from across the street. He could see Penny writing furiously, her shoulders moving up and down with each new line.

"Won't be a problem." Beck checked his watch. It was 4:06 p.m.

"Good," Tony replied. "Talk to you soon."

Beck reached up and hit the smallest button on his earpiece which turned the mic off. He removed it, putting it in his pocket. He took a deep breath. He wasn't afraid or nervous because he was walking up to a girl. He was anxious because he felt the weight of the world sinking through his organs, and he hoped he had the strength to keep them afloat. As Binta's soft kindness floated into his mind, he hoped he had the courage to do the right thing. In one breath, Beck walked up to the door, opened it, and as best as he could, walked casually over to where Penny was sitting, deep in thought and deep in her writing. He sat down across from her. She looked up and back down in one motion, and never stopped writing. Annoyance flashed across her eyes.

"Can I help you?" she asked. Beck was surprised by the authority in her voice. It spoke from her mind, not her heart. Momentarily he wondered how that wall had been built.

Beck tried to match her energy. "Yes, actually you can." His tone came off much too serious. Penny put down her pen, like one of the ones you find in a hotel, and folded over her brown leather notebook. She crossed her arms on top of it and leaned forward, staring into his eyes. Beck was taken aback by their beauty, but more so by the sincerity of their strength.

"How exactly?" she replied firmly. She really wasn't interested.

Beck surprised himself with how well he kept it together. "I need you to listen to me. I work for the government. Well, kind of, and…"

"Let me stop you there, I don't fuck with the government, okay?"

"Well you're going to have to fuck with the government really soon or shit is going to hit the fan for you and the rest of the world."

Penny didn't say anything. She just stared. Beck took a deep breath. This was not how he intended things to go. He thought he'd ask her out for dinner and break it to her slowly, but here they were.

Beck brought his voice to a near whisper, "I need you to listen to me very carefully, Penny."

"How do you know my name? Who the hell are you?" She started to get up, but Beck grabbed her hands. He looked deep into her eyes, and she looked back, slowly allowing him to pull her back down into her seat.

"Just listen, please. And keep your voice down. My name is Becker Brooks, and I am here to protect you. You are in danger. The government is after your mind and I need to make sure they don't get to you."

"My mind? Also, I don't need anyone to protect me. Thanks."

"Right. Sorry. This isn't real, where we are right now. Well it is real and it's important, but it's an alternate construction of reality created by your thoughts and memories. This isn't present day."

"It's not October 1976?"

"Well *here* it is, in this memory — your memory. But I'm from October 1979. I've been watching over you for a few years of your time now, and it's time we actually met. Things are going to start getting interesting."

"I don't follow. Why should I trust you?"

"Well, do you?"

"Do I what?"

"Trust me?" Their eye contact had been steady, and Penny's wall of cynicism crumbled ever so slightly. She did trust him, though she didn't understand why. She narrowed her eyes to slits. "Until you give me a reason not to."

"Great. I'll explain more, but we need to leave here. Do you know of somewhere safe?" A few men in suits were glancing their way in line for coffee and Beck needed to be sure. He reached over and pulled the navy blue hood of her jacket over her head. She tried to swat his hand away.

"Don't touch me."

"Sorry," Beck said. "Where can we go?"

"My place, I guess? Don't get the wrong idea."

"Wouldn't think of it." He winked at her. "That's not safe though. Anywhere else?"

"I guess the train tracks by the water. There's a small cliff overhang."

"Great, how far is that?"

"Just down the street."

He didn't think she'd let him grab her hand so he didn't try. They stood and walked casually to the door. Beck checked to ensure the men didn't follow. Once they were outside and walking, Beck noticed Penny's slight limp. He hesitated to ask, because he knew what had happened, but she didn't know he knew. He wanted to say all the right things.

"What happened to your leg?"

"I'd rather not talk about it, thanks."

"Okay, I'm sorry."

Penny felt a tinge of guilt. She was being extremely curt to someone who was seemingly trying to help her. "I was in a car accident when I was really young. I lost my leg."

"I'm sorry," Beck replied honestly. "You don't have to talk about it."

"It's okay. You haven't proven otherwise yet."

"Good to hear. Glad I've lasted five minutes."

Penny smiled softly. She noticed it was the first time she'd smiled and laughed in a while. She was so consumed by her work and her writing that she hadn't given herself permission to feel. She'd been content with her fierce, cynical independence, ignoring her loneliness for decades. She hadn't yet realized that she didn't have to be alone to save herself, and write what she needed to write. She wrote for others, for the things she saw, and from the heart of her memory. For a moment, she wondered if she could bookmark this interaction as something she could write for herself.

Penny and Beck walked along the foggy street and turned left onto another which they followed all the way to the water. The trees lining the street guided them with a vividness that Beck hadn't seen before. Was this how Penny saw them? The colours were smeared beautifully like an oil painting against the dimming grey sky. Penny closed her eyes and breathed in the damp air. They walked in silence for some time before Penny told him they were at the water. They walked to a hidden stone stairway on the other side of the train tracks, down to the beach. Beck went first, and was worried Penny would have trouble with the steepness and unevenness of this staircase, but when he offered his hand, she shoved it away. Once they reached the bottom, they sat under the cliff overhang beside the staircase, facing the waves. The sun was setting, but all you could see was a stripe of yellow extending out toward them on the water. The sky progressively darkened in shades of grey, matching the colours of the waves. It looked like a black-and-white photograph.

After a few moments of silence, Penny interrupted, "So, what now?" She looked at Beck. He could tell she was trying to be nonchalant, but detected a hint of fear in her voice. She wasn't as confident now as she had first seemed.

"Well, I'm not entirely sure. I'm just following orders from my boss. He said I need to protect you."

Penny rolled her eyes. "Well I think I'm pretty protected now," she replied sarcastically, referring to their location. "Could you explain what exactly is going on?"

"You have no idea how fast they can find you," Beck answered, "and, yeah, I suppose now is a good time." Beck wasn't sure how much he could tell her. Would this alter her memories too much? He reached into his pocket and put his earpiece in, turning on the mic.

"Hello?" Beck called into it. Tony had instructed Beck not to mention his name. He told him that he didn't want too much on Penny's mind, but in reality, Tony couldn't risk Penny finding out it was him, or Beck finding out the past just yet.

"What are you doing?" Penny asked. Beck motioned "one second" with his finger.

"Hey, kid, how is everything going?" Tony replied at the other end.

"Quick question. How much can I tell her?"

"Is she there with you now?" Tony asked, desperately trying to hide the shake of emotion in his voice. He was anxious, nervous, sad, excited, and happy all at once. He wanted nothing more than to hear Penny's voice.

"Uh, yeah, she's here, that's why I'm asking." Beck replied somewhat sarcastically. He could sense something off in Tony's voice.

"You can explain. I'm watching the monitor." Tony had a hold of his voice now.

"Who is that? Can I talk to them? Will *they* tell me what the hell's going on?" Penny asked Beck, a little impatiently now.

Tony was frozen on the other end. He'd heard her. "Yeah, she can talk to me if she wants. I guess that's easier," he replied. He had no idea what he was going to say or if he was going to be able to keep it together. He prayed that she wouldn't recognize his voice. Beck took out his earpiece and handed it to Penny, who held it for a moment, examining it.

"Interesting," she noted before trying to put it in her ear. Beck reached over to help but she swatted his hand away again. After a few moments of trying, she let Beck help her. He reached over, putting her hair behind her ear, and clipped the earpiece on. They made eye contact and she looked away, but Beck didn't. He couldn't pinpoint what exactly it was that he felt. He watched her gather herself and mutter, "Hello?"

Tony didn't respond for a few moments, long enough that Penny asked again, "Hello?"

Tony was shaking. Hearing Penny's voice again lit his heart up. "Hi, Penny," he managed.

"Who are you?"

"It's better if you don't know."

"You sound familiar."

"I'm not," Tony answered a little too quickly.

"Sounds like you are."

"I'm not. A lot of voices sound alike."

"Right, well, could you tell me what's going on, please? This person you sent wasn't much help." She looked over at Beck, rolling her eyes. There was a pause at the other end. Tony was dumbfounded, and unsure of what he could tell her without breaking.

"Can you?" Penny insisted.

"I'll do my best, Pen."

"What did you call me?" Penny demanded, her voice cracking slightly.

"Sorry, habit. I knew another girl named Penny."

"All right." She paused. Tony was sure she knew.

"Here's what you do need to know."

#

Beck and Penny sat under the rock for about an hour after Tony had explained things. Penny, being Penny, had asked every possible question. Tony explained what Beck had to do, which was met with an assertive request to protect herself. Tony told her that she couldn't easily protect herself because she wouldn't see the Sifters coming in earlier memories. Penny accepted this reluctantly. Tony explained everything else the same way he had to Beck, though without disclosing his and Paul's names. Beck thought this odd, along with Penny's gaze out into the water. She wasn't afraid. She was sad and pained as if Tony's voice hurt her in and of itself. Beck knew she knew something that he didn't. She would have been more terrified by the nature of what was happening around her if she didn't.

Beck was quiet. He didn't know what Tony had chosen to tell her, and thus he didn't say anything. Penny was quiet too, now, and Beck didn't want to pry. She'd taken off her prosthetic leg, and sat hugging her other knee. It was dark now, but they didn't start a fire. The navy blue and white water rolled over itself against the black sky, which was littered with stars.

"He said to trust you," Penny said, finally breaking the silence and looking at Beck. He could still see how light her eyes were, as they reflected the moonlight.

"And do you?"

Penny shifted her weight. She thought for a moment. She did trust what he was telling her. But she didn't want to be protected, or saved. She didn't want to be the hero she now needed to be, defying some kind of odds. She wrote because she could hardly walk. She just wanted to live.

"I trust that you'll do the right thing," she finally spoke.

Her words lifted Beck's heart more than he expected. He just nodded.

"You know, you don't have to be afraid of saying the wrong thing."

Beck looked at her. He was confused. "Why not?"

"Because it's not about you. Just be here."

Beck nodded again. "Okay, I will." He meant it. Penny knew he did too.

"Why do you suppose it's us. It doesn't make sense that it's us."

"What do you mean?"

"Well, there's all of this generational trauma, history, and these stories inside us, especially you. I mean, we don't really know, but there could be. If it's not about us, then why us? It feels odd for it to be us." Beck was thinking of Binta.

"Because they're stories we can't fully understand?"

"Well," Beck paused a moment, "yeah."

Penny wasn't sure how to answer. She thought for a moment, looking up at the stars, all composed of the same gasses and fire. Her fingers itched for a pen. There was a book inside her. Come to think of it, there was probably a book inside everyone.

"I suppose, that just because it isn't about us, doesn't mean it's not our problem. I think setting these stories free is our burden to bear. We're not telling them, we're just giving them a chance to be out there, running their natural course."

Beck nodded. Her words struck him in a way he couldn't comprehend. He thought it might have been love, but it wasn't the type of love he expected.

"So, you're a writer?"

"Yeah, I guess you could call it that," Penny responded quietly. Beck could feel the pain in her past radiating off of her. He inched a little closer, and Penny looked at him coldly.

"Why do you write?" Beck asked.

Nobody had ever asked her this before. "Because I can't not do it." Her response was firmer than she'd intended. "My mother died a scientist. So I thought I'd die a writer." She smiled at Beck, trying to break some of tension. It dawned on her that this might have been the longest conversation she'd had in a while. Beck smiled back, but she could tell he was still unsure what to say.

"My mom used to read me Proverbs. Which was odd for a scientist. But I used to picture her as Lady Wisdom. I would have followed her anywhere. She told me that we take our chances for wonder for granted in science — always trying to get ahead, always hijacking, manipulating."

"I didn't take you for someone who lives to wonder."

"Nobody does. Why would you when I've been through what I have."

Beck shook his head. "That's the reason you have, *because* you've been through so much."

"Maybe," Penny paused. "I guess I write what I choose to notice."

Beck looked around him and smiled. "Well, you notice a lot. So hopefully I'll have some good books to read soon."

Penny smiled weakly. As hard as Penny's shell was, she was afraid. She could smell darkness. It was like the heavy smell of damp cold. Beck opened his arms. She hesitated for a moment, before shifting over to him.

She knew all he wanted to do was comfort her. She breathed in. He smelled like warm chicory root.

"Don't be sorry." She looked up at him.

"The further I go back, the more answers you're going to have. The more it's going to make sense. I promise."

"But I won't know you each time."

"Eventually you will, and you will come looking for answers."

"Outside my memories?"

"Yeah."

There was pain, of a past Beck would later learn on the many trips he made back to this time to speak with her about what little she remembered of her mother, not knowing her father and the finiteness of their lives. They would sit in silence mostly, comforted by each other's presence, learning to love again beyond the archetypes of it. Beck usually stayed awake staring thoughtfully out into the thick blue water and sky, which were almost inseparable unless you concentrated.

#

They lay under the rocks at dawn, a now familiar occurrence. Each time Beck sifted, he returned to this moment. He was sifting nearly every day now, as time ran short. For Beck, Tony, and Paul it was late November 1979. Beck found himself living for these small pieces of 1976.

Penny rested her head on Beck's chest as she wrote. They figured that it was the safest to be together at sundown or sun-up. She was now finishing a fiction arts master's program, and Beck refused to tell her if her poetry or fiction had been published over the next few years, which aggravated her.

"Would you read it to me?" he asked, pulling her long strands of hair out of her face as the wind swept them every which way.

"Absolutely not," she answered sternly. "This one isn't finished yet."

"Read me what you have?"

Penny sighed and tossed her pen into her lap. She smoothed out the paper of her notebook and read:

"*Your mind is,*
as genius has partially determined,

unapologetically the opposite of black and white.
It's more like black and blue,
but neither one or the other,
perpetually bruised by life,
for those gifted with ambition
and restless, chaotically cyclical thoughts.
The hour turns an eerie fresh mint blue
after it has been happy for a few,
and in its wake,
a slowly bruising sky
mocks and calls to unheard delicate minds,
and the vulnerable scars unseen,
as red and purple swirl into
tomorrow's yellow and green."

"It's beautiful, Pen."

"Thanks…" Her sentence trailed off as both of them paused to watch the first colours of the day crash over one another in the waves. Beck noticed another notebook in her bag. It looked like a calendar. Penny turned and saw him looking at it. She fished it out of her bookbag and handed it to him. It was old, made of some sort of cross between paper and cloth, and exactly seventy-two pages long. It had beautiful paintings above the few days noted on each page.

"It's a Japanese calendar. My mom got it for me at a market in Seattle when I was little. The year is split into seventy-two sections."

"Did you paint these?"

"I did. It was really hard — each of the sections are so specific, and usually only a few days."

"Takes some incredible observation skills."

"Well that's what's intriguing about it, I think. No two people would have painted it the same way. I'm more optimistic than I'd like to admit, that my writing or painting might be taken as a trustworthy observation one day, like science."

Beck took her words much deeper into his mind than he'd expected. She was right. He thought of himself, Tony, Paul, and science. Penny was an observer, and you can't be an objective one. He thought about whose observations the world chose to trust. It dawned on him that whoever was orchestrating the natural movements of essences had chosen to trust Penny. Beck smiled down at her. She tilted her chin up so her eyes could meet his gaze, and smiled weakly back. You don't always need electric speeches to light the fire of a revolution. Sometimes you just need two twigs willing to listen to and feel the wind.

CHAPTER 11

– Observe –

December 1979, Kingston, New Jersey

O n his way to Tony's house, Beck stopped at a small, family-owned bookstore.

"Excuse me, sir, where's the poetry section?" he asked the cashier.

"In the back to the left."

"Thanks." Beck made his way to the back between the narrow passages created by the shelves. The place smelled old and comfortable and was filled with villages of ideas, migrations of thoughts, and theatres of memories. Penny spoke of ideas often, and where they came from. She said, "In a world where ideas seem scarce, it was an honour to find one, or rather, be given one." He didn't really understand what it meant, but he liked the way she stood by it. He began running his fingers across the spines of the books, searching the shelves for a name. Penny had always said she would publish under something generic, so he tried Smith and Brown, but there was no Pen, Penny, or Penelope. *Where are you, Pen?* He went back through again, and paused abruptly, his forefinger resting on the top of a navy blue book, patterned with familiar grey waves of endless water. It was as if she'd made it so he'd find it. He tilted it off the shelf into his palms. It was thin, maybe one hundred pages of poems, and titled *Art Imitating Science Imitating Art*. Beck's hands shook, as he opened the book to the first poem:

The Blue Hour
Your mind is,
as genius has partially determined,
unapologetically the opposite of black and white.
It's more like black and blue,
but neither one or the other,
perpetually bruised by life,
for those gifted with ambition
and restless, chaotically cyclical thoughts.
The hour turns an eerie fresh mint blue
after it has been happy for a few,
and in its wake,
a slowly bruising sky
mocks and calls to unheard delicate minds,
and the vulnerable scars unseen,
as red and purple swirl into
tomorrow's yellow and green.

Beck was taken aback by the power in the words, even after having heard them a few days prior. He noticed that the poem was unedited and unchanged, which surprised him, given that Penny had written it three years earlier. She had mentioned that she didn't edit much. As she'd wrestled with her fate, she'd come to believe that memories were moments of energy, ones she didn't wish to tatter or fracture. She believed in building good memories, and though she only spoke those words recently, had always felt this way. Telling the truth was art in and of itself. They belonged in their raw form. Beck smiled, holding the book gently in his hands. He was about to place it back on the shelf, when he caught the peculiar pseudonym on the cover. It read: *Susanna Brown.*

#

They could feel each other's bodies shaking. Their breathing was just set-tling back down. Beck looked down and only then realized how tiny her hand was in his. He glanced at his watch: December 23, 1953.

"Mr. Beck?" the little voice said, looking up with a brightness Beck didn't recognize in her. "What are we doing?"

"Pen, we've got to play hide-and-seek for a bit." He felt even more inclined to protect her in her younger years.

"Mr. Anthony calls me Pen."

"What?"

"He calls me Pen too."

"Who's Mr. Anthony?" Beck looked at her as intensely as his stomach drowned. Her black hair was longer than she would keep it years later, before she would fill with apathy and turn against the world, before she lost her leg, and before her heart was cleaved. Beck still couldn't put words to how her brokenness was destined to heal the world. One day, maybe Penny would. Her arms were wrapped around her knees as they sat in the cold alley. The brick felt like solid ice against their thinly coated backs. Her wavy curls fell around her shoulders and skinny arms, as if it were an extra blanket — a warmth she would chop off because it reminded her of too much. She thought herself tougher by needing less. Beck always thought she looked strikingly like Snow White, a century before her, but this time with many more tools and a mind filled with lives that weren't lived, as if the weight of their memories rode on her shoulders and whispered their stories, and for the first time, not falling on deaf ears. These stories literally expanded through her mind.

"Tell me about Mr. Anthony." Beck reached up and turned off his earpiece.

"He's a really smart doctor and I wish he was my daddy. I think he's Mommy's best friend. Mommy told me she loves him, but not in a daddy way. She said she loves someone else in a daddy way but he doesn't come visit very much."

It couldn't be, Beck thought. Tony had told him that he had no personal stake in all this. Beck was sure Tony had told him everything, but now he needed answers. Something dawned on him. Why was he back this far in Penny's past anyway? He knew her memories were more vulnerable here. She couldn't ward off the Sifters as easily. She didn't understand that they were coming. Regardless, Beck felt that something was off. He looked around the corner of the wall. There didn't seem to be anything out of the ordinary. Penny started humming.

"Shhh!"

"Sorry, sorry, sorry." Penny cupped her red mittens over her mouth, her eyes open wide. Beck peered out of the alley to make sure no one was coming.

"It's okay," Beck assured her. "How far away is your house from here?"

"It takes me ten whole minutes to walk."

"Okay, we need to go, now."

"Why? What's wrong?"

"I need to know some things."

"About Mommy?"

Beck looked at her sharply. "Yes, Pen. Do you know what she does?"

"She works with Mr. Anthony, but she says I'm not allowed to know any more than that."

"Does she call him Mr. Anthony?"

"No, she calls him Tony. Mr. Anthony wants me to call him Tony too, but I think Mr. Anthony makes him sound more like a smart scientist."

Beck sat back against the wall and put his hands on the top of his head, craning his neck to look up at the falling snow. He felt the onset of panic. He knew Penny's mother died tomorrow, but he never would have guessed that her mother was Susanna. Tony must have sent him here for a reason. He wasn't one to disregard the repercussions either. Beck felt like he was driving blind. All this had already happened — they were Penny's memories — but he had no idea what to do next. He looked across at Penny who was staring at him, confused.

"What's wrong, Mr. Beck?"

"Nothing, it's okay. We just need to go."

"You said that already. I'm waiting for *you*."

Beck looked at her and smiled. He saw where her sarcasm came from now. He put his hood up.

"Put your hood up. We can't be seen."

#

Once in the house, Beck told Penny to play as if he wasn't there, in case Susanna came in. He told her he had important detective work to do, which was how he explained things to her when he sifted her memories at this age. This task was going to be difficult because everything in the house was constructed based off of her memory. Tony had explained that memories were sometimes more vivid when the person was young because they were firsts — there weren't a lot of other memories clouding them. *He's so full of shit*, Beck thought. Beck couldn't see anything. The only thing that was really vivid was the red-and-purple stained glass window in the kitchen. Penny had told him that Susanna's office was behind the kitchen, so that's where he headed, quietly. He had sent Penny in to check and make sure Susanna wasn't home. He assumed Penny had never really been in the office, so the memories she had of it would be far and few between. He opened the beautiful wooden door, which he noticed was similar to the one Tony and Paul's office had at Princeton. Under different circumstances, he would have been thrilled to step foot in such a beautiful house.

"Come on, Pen, work with me," he whispered under his breath. Anything he needed to find, anything confidential, he had no hope of seeing clearly. Penny would never have seen it. All he could do was search for the odd thing she might have seen. He saw a desk, a beautiful purple-and-red rug on the wall, and matching curtains on the small window of the door to the backyard. The office was clean. Susanna must have been Tony's saving grace in that sense. He walked over to her desk, straining to see something that looked like words, but most of it appeared as blank paper with muffled lines of black ink.

"Damn it." The only thing that was clear was a photograph of Susanna, Paul, and Tony with their arms around one another. They were sitting in an old blue car — the same one in the photograph in Paul and Tony's office. He wondered why they didn't have this one. There were charts on the walls with lines and blurred out numbers. *What am I looking for?* There was still something missing. Beck sat in Susanna's chair and put his head in his hands. *Think, Beck*, he thought. He heard a key begin to slide into the lock in the back door to his left. He panicked and leapt behind the large set of shelves on the hinge side of the door. The phone began ringing as Susanna walked in. She grumbled as she put all her belongings on her desk, and picked it up angrily. *How am I seeing and hearing this if Penny isn't here?* Beck thought. Tony had more explaining to do.

"Wow you wasted no time... yes I said I'd be home at noon... Mark, it's 12:03 calm down." She turned and glanced back at the clock on the wall behind her. "No, I can't come to D.C. tomorrow, it's Christmas Eve... right I forgot you're a heartless prick. You'd know if you had kids... no, I don't know anything about it... yes, I worked with them in college... no... I *was* living with them but I have no idea if they are doing something illegal... well if they are, and I knew about it, don't you think I would have told you... oh really... we're... we *were* engaged. That's past tense... you know, Mark, I have work to do, it's my Thursday afternoon, okay... yeah, okay... I don't know what you're talking about... well if you think I do, that's too bad... no they won't be here for Christmas. Past tense, remember? Okay bye... shit." Susanna hung up the phone by slamming it down on the receiver. She ran her fingers through her hair, dug her nails into her scalp, and slammed her palms on the table. Her tone changed abruptly, streaked with worry. "Shit."

Beck's thoughts were spinning. He had wondered why Paul and Tony were working in D.C. and she was living in Salem. She had been working with them? They'd kept all the details of these relationships from him. The question now was if she knew about their little side project and what her involvement was in it. Beck didn't know whether to trust her. At this time, Mark would have known that Paul and Tony were up to something. Was Susanna saying she didn't know anything because she was afraid for Penny's safety? Which one of them was she engaged to? It had to be Tony. The phone rang again, and Susanna answered it hastily.

"What? ...Oh, sorry, Tony." Beck clasped his hands over his mouth trying to conceal how heavily he was breathing. Susanna glanced around the room, as if she could sense him there. *How?* Beck thought.

"You already know I don't think that's a good idea... yeah I know you want to see her... no I don't think... Tony... all right please come alone and make sure no one knows... yeah, he did... he thinks I know something and I can't keep telling him I don't. I've got blueprints in my office.

You need to take them back with you… okay, fine, I'll see you tomorrow… yeah… bye."

Beck stood in that corner for what felt like hours with his hands clapped over his mouth. *Tony, what the hell.* Susanna finally stood and left her office through the kitchen, finding Penny sitting on a stool at the kitchen counter, colouring a Christmas catalogue.

"What are you up to?" Susanna breathed out, clearly hoping to hear a good response.

"I heard you yelling." Penny didn't look up. Beck stepped out from behind the bookshelves and stood in the middle of the room, waiting for Penny to look up.

"It's okay, just work stuff. I'm sorry you heard it." She smiled lovingly and reached out to rub Penny's shoulders. Penny looked up and slightly past her mother to check for Beck, who waved. Penny nodded subtly and he disappeared. Susanna snapped her head around to look back into her office.

"Who are you nodding at?"

"You."

"Why were you looking back there?"

"I don't know, kids do strange things, don't they?" She looked up and smiled at her mother, who smiled back and pulled her in for a hug. Susanna was nervous. For a moment she fearfully entertained the thought, that in the future, Tony and Paul had figured out what they were working on. She knew someone had been standing in her office and glanced out to the kitchen window to the backyard, at the roses. She turned back to Penny colouring. "Why do you still have your jacket on?"

Penny shrugged, skipping toward the door. A piece of paper fell from the pocket as she hung up her coat. It read:

Call me when you remember this memory in 1979.

609-144-2550

Beck

Perfect squares. That's how she'd remember it twenty-five years later.

#

Beck woke up in Tony's office. He sat up, throwing the lid of the APM open.

"We're going to the pub," he spoke sternly and aggressively, though still a little disoriented. He tugged off the wires that were attached to his face, neck, and chest.

"Hey, woah, be careful. What did I say about turning your mic off?"

"Why? Because I'll break your stupid machine?"

"No, because you could get hurt, Beck. What the hell?"

"We're going to the pub," Beck shot back coldly.

"All right, okay," Tony answered. "Get your coat on and calm down."

Tony waited at the front door and handed Beck his coat. Beck didn't take it.

"Don't need it," he said sharply, forcing direct eye contact. Tony knew Beck knew something, and he was afraid of what it was. This time was bound to come, though he thought he had more time.

#

In the pub, three silent snowy miles from the house, Tony and Beck sat across from one another in a booth. Tony was watching Beck spin his third beer's cap in his hands. Tony had had three glasses of scotch. Neither of them had said a word yet.

"Beck."

"What?"

"Well shit, I don't know, that's the point!"

"You've got a lot to tell me, huh?"

Tony was silent.

"You were there when Susanna died, weren't you? She was working with you? Penny is her daughter? You were engaged? Anything else I should fucking know, doctor?"

Tony looked down as unwanted rage circled in his eyes.

"Uhm," Tony muttered, his voice cracking, "no, she was engaged to Paul."

"What the actual fuck?"

"Yeah, Becker, what the actual fuck, huh?"

"I didn't mean it like that."

Tony just shook his head. "You know what, Brooks? Maybe you *were* the wrong person for this job. You were. And now I'm going to pay for it on too many damn levels."

"Take it outside, mate!" the Australian bartender yelled from the other side of the room.

"Fuck off, Chris!" Tony yelled back. He put his head in his hands, his elbows resting on the plastic gloss coating of the wooden table. The lights were dim enough that you really couldn't see faces well, especially if you were drunk.

"Tony, I didn't know."

"No, Beck you didn't know, and I wanted it to stay that way."

"How the hell can you keep something like that from me, and ask me to do what I'm doing?"

"Because if I don't tell you everything then I don't have to accept the truth of what I *really* don't want to tell you."

"Lovely. And what would that be?"

"Can I get another scotch and another Corona, Chris?" Tony's blood-shot, damp eyes slowly wandered back to meet Beck's. They both felt something, which had been unspoken until this moment.

"I care about you, kid. And I don't think I can bear to lose you too."

"Too?"

"I lost Susanna. I couldn't save her. The crash killed her instantly." He wiped the tears from his eyes in a way that almost seemed like he was dismissive of the events, but Beck knew it was an act. Not unlike everything else to this point.

"And Penny?"

"Yes, I was there. I pulled her out, made sure she was safe in the hospital and I left."

"Do you realize how much she adored you?"

"Do *you* realize how much I adored her?"

"Then why?"

"Because on paper, Paul is her father."

"What the hell do you mean *on paper*?"

"She's mine, technically, but Paul thinks she's his. The only one alive who knows is me. And, well, you now."

Beck sat back in the booth, looking up at the ceiling. "Wow, so she lived with her grandmother all this time, thinking she has no parents alive while you two hide out here in the country doing all this? You're getting me to go through her memories and you're not going to tell her anything? She hasn't seen you in decades and you just treat her like another experiment that *you* want to do *by yourself* behind the government's back because you think you're better than them?"

"No, Beck, that's not true. And you know it."

"Bullshit."

"Mr. Brooks, did it ever occur to you that you weren't the only one who cared about Penny? And that someone in your life actually cares about you? This is the continuation of humanity at stake. I made a choice. I made a choice for humanity over my own damn daughter! How do you think that feels? Huh?"

"And me?" Beck cut him off.

Tony paused, holding Beck's gaze.

"Beck, believe it or not there's much more I should tell you."

Beck didn't move, he just looked back. He had nothing more to say. Tony owed him these answers.

"Sifters are recruited, yes, because they have little to no apparent connection to life or major family ties, but there's another reason."

Beck was still silent, staring blankly.

"Chris, where are my drinks?" Tony demanded.

"Right here, calm down." Chris slammed them down on the table and walked away. Tony waited until he was far enough away to continue.

"Essences are only visible, and we can only access them when that person is within one year of their death. It's almost as if there is a predetermined expiry date, but we figured out how to see it. Something or someone seems to know and dictate when people are going to die. You've seen the maps — there's a very specific countdown. Now, essences can connect with other essences, which is what the Sifters do, and what you're doing..." His sentence trailed off as he paused, seeing the hurt building across the table. "Beck, listen, I..."

Beck's eyes were tearing with an unfamiliar anger. "And so I'm just another one of them for you, huh? A disposable pawn. I'm going to die.

That's what you're telling me? And so is Penny? And you're doing damn near nothing about it?"

"Beck, what *can* I do about it? I know which memories would save you and that aches like hell. I know because I sit downstairs all night watching them for you both, and it breaks me. Stopping someone from dying involves manipulating memories too, and it changes the person. It also causes a whole myriad of butterfly effects. Think about what it would cost for everyone else if I made another selfish choice. It might break the world, for good."

"You didn't tell me though. Why the fuck didn't you just tell me?" Beck was still confused. *Why does it have to be me?*

"Because I care about you. Can't you see that?" Tony yelled at him. "My mistake!"

"Yeah, mine too." Beck stood and smashed his beer against the wall. "How dare you?" He stormed out of the bar, leaving his coat behind.

Tony waited a few seconds and stood to walk after him.

"You're going to have to clean that up, Crypt." Chris had grabbed Tony's arm.

"Try me." Tony sneered into his gruff, unshaven face, and pulled his arm free. He walked out the front door of the bar and called after Beck.

"Brooks, you're going to freeze yourself to death out here. Let me drive you back to the house and then you can go road rage all over the damn place!" There was no answer. "Dammit," he muttered through his already chattering teeth.

Tony shoved his hands into his pockets and stood looking out at the street, which hadn't been plowed. The lamplights formed yellow cones of visible snowfall, illuminating the gas station across the street. There was nothing else for miles, and Tony felt a small pang of worry. *Where would I have gone*, he thought. He threw Beck's jacket over his shoulders without putting the arms on, shoved his hands further into his pockets, and jogged across the street.

CHAPTER 12

– Lift –

December 1979, Kingston, New Jersey

Tony leaned against the wall of the gas station until Beck sauntered out with four boxes of candy and a pack of cigarettes.

"Thought you didn't smoke."

"Don't talk to me," Beck sneered and started walking away. The anger that had been accumulating in his heart since he was a kid was now trying to burst through the cold dry cracks in his skin.

"You're going to walk three miles by yourself back to the house in the blizzard?" Tony replied sarcastically. The snow was falling faster and creating a thick barrier between their voices, so he had to shout. Beck didn't reply. Tony rolled his eyes and trudged across the street to the pub and got in his car. He turned the keys in the ignition and tried to back out of the lot, but there was so much snow that the wheels wouldn't go through it. He sat with both hands on the steering wheel, shoulders shrugged up, and miserably drunk. He growled in frustration, and at what he wasn't entirely sure, but it was because he knew deep down that he had screwed up again, and done so badly. He climbed out of the car and slammed the door, shoving the keys into his pocket so hard that he heard the stitching crack. He'd have to go for a walk to get the car in the morning. Or he'd send Paul to do it. No, he'd do it.

Tony needed to catch up with Beck before he lost sight of him in the blizzard. They were both drunk, so that didn't help. Tony had held in the things he desperately needed to tell him for too long. Silence was often more telling. Tony jogged in the direction that Beck went, pain searing through his body, even through the alcohol. Another item on the list to tell Beck. There came a time when alcohol stopped forwarding everything to tomorrow. He kept jogging as the cold ripped through him. Beck couldn't have been walking this fast. Tony had only been to the car for a few minutes. He looked around and could hardly see anything around him except the rare street light illuminating the speed and thickness of the snowfall.

"Beck!" Tony called.

A snowball the size of a grapefruit hit him square in the chest. It came from across the road and Tony strained his eyes to see. He'd never been so happy to have the wind knocked out of him. He jogged across the street to find Beck walking somberly and shivering uncomfortably.

"Put your damn coat on." Tony shoved it at him. This time Beck took it.

"Thought you were driving."

"I was, but the car is stuck in the fucking snow. The wheels won't move. I'm also drunk and it's blizzarding."

"How the hell did you find me?"

"Funny."

"What?"

"You threw a snowball through my lungs."

"Definitely didn't."

Tony didn't answer. He figured Beck was messing with him. It did occur to him that he never would have found him otherwise.

"We need to talk," Tony muttered, almost hoping that Beck wouldn't hear him. He had zipped his coat up to his nose and was speaking through it.

"No shit," Beck replied. He still hadn't put his arms through the sleeves of his jacket. He wrapped it around himself like a blanket. The truth was, Beck didn't want to believe Tony. He was terrified. But, in an odd way he felt he didn't need to be, even if what Tony had told him was true. Beck had never feared death — he never felt that he had much to lose, but he'd been afraid of leaving people behind. Now, he was afraid of leaving the memories untold, encased like amber in essences. They each deserved to be set free — whether traumatic, triumphant, or examples of love, no matter where they came from. They deserved the chance to freely flow between generations, their paths unadulterated, unmanipulated, and alive. A memory, though it can be false, holds the potential to be someone's truth and meaning in the mind to which it is meant to be passed and unlocked. He had to help Penny and it dawned on him that he had to help Tony too. Tony had given him friendship, guidance, and a purpose. He now knew Tony had a dark and troubled past, and made poor decisions in the midst of it. Beck realized that Tony's actions were beyond repenting his sins. He could no longer sit still silently — silence had eaten and withered his body. Tony was trying to save the world though he wasn't its savior. The savior wasn't Beck either, or even Penny. Nobody, individually or as a group was. Tony had been moved by something outside of himself — something that should continue to expand as the universe does and as essences do: love, with the promise of loss, through the son he never had, the daughter he tried to protect, the best friend he couldn't live without, and the woman who taught him patience. His story wasn't one that was unique to him, nor was it common. Beck didn't know if it was the cold or the alcohol making him so sentimentally aware, but he thought about his own mind, picturing a small bucket within it. It was filled with memories that were not his, whether they were stories of a history he'd been led to believe or the truth in the past. He felt he knew how to separate and sort through them, and that somehow he always had. He just needed to do it. Penny was so striking that something or someone had decided to splay her essence out over the Earth, but perhaps more importantly, the essences she'd been trusted to carry, woven through her own. There wasn't just one destination like the others either. There was no guidance beyond this at all. It was simply a choice to trust.

"Well, we've got about an hour of walking so I'm just going to say some things. You don't have to answer."

Tears were streaming down Beck's face but there was so much snow you couldn't tell the difference. He stopped and turned to look at Tony, who walked a few more steps before realizing Beck had stopped. He turned too, and Beck could see the look in his eyes. Tony didn't know what to do, and he never did. They were more alike than they realized, and they both knew then that they didn't know what defined duty until they met one another, until Penny bridged the gap between them and until love bridged the gap between duty and being human. Beck looked down, feeling slightly embarrassed and uneasy. He was still drunk. He didn't look up when he heard Tony's boots in the snow take the few steps toward him and wrap him in a hug. Beck buried his face into Tony's jacket and cried. The more Beck's shoulders launched up and down with waves of aching sobs, the tighter Tony held him, and eventually, he put his hands over the back of Beck's head and repeated, "It's okay, it's okay. I've got you." They both forgot they were cold as the snow swirled frantically around them in the black night. Tony looked up at the sky, eyes closed.

After a few moments, Beck raised his head and wiped his face with his hands.

"I'm listening."

They began walking again, as if nothing had happened, but care was no longer unspoken. The newfound energy in their pace proved it.

"You have questions?"

"I just need to let it sit."

"Okay."

"Susanna. Is that why…?"

"Partially. Her death was motivation. Our parents' deaths were motivation. Protecting Penny was motivation. It was a combination of a lot of things that didn't get us anywhere until we looked beyond them." Tony was speaking in rapid succession, but he caught himself. He paused for a moment before continuing, "Beck, I'm sorry I didn't tell you everything. I've had to make a lot of choices. I didn't always make the right ones."

"No one says you have to."

"I should have told you the details but I didn't trust you to stay if I did."

"I've felt so alone my whole life. I'd stay just because I wasn't alone."

Tony smiled, feeling the cold in his cheeks fighting against it. "There's one more thing. Susanna."

"You worked with her? She's Penny's mother, right? And you're…"

"Her father, yes. But it's about Susanna's essence."

"What about it?"

"I knew there was a reason I liked you so much."

Beck stopped walking. "Me? But how?"

"Your guess is as good as mine. I'm not surprised though."

"Is that why I can see things Penny hasn't? Like Susanna's office? And her phone call with Mark?" Beck looked away. *Shit*. He hadn't planned to bring that up just yet.

"Possibly, yes. I don't know. We don't know how essences are used by the people who inherit them." Tony was quiet for a few moments as he thought about this, but he quickly remembered what Beck had said. "What phone call with Mark? Why were you in her office?"

"I don't know why." Beck's voice trailed off. He wasn't sure now was the time.

"Yes, you do."

Beck froze. *Shit.* "I was just following Penny."

"No you weren't. Don't shit me, Brooks." Tony stopped and stared hard at him.

"I don't know anything!"

"You were *there* the day before she died. What did you see?"

"Oh is that why you sent me there?"

"Partially, yes."

"More lies."

"I didn't lie, I just didn't tell you."

"Among a growing list of other things."

"Knock it off."

"Make me."

"Becker, what did you see?" Tony sounded worried and impatient now.

Beck looked down. He felt the snow, breathing cold down his neck. "She was on the phone with Mark, before you called that day. He threatened her."

"In Salem?" There was panic in Tony's voice.

"Yeah. I think something was planned."

"Well I can see that now." Tony stopped and put his head in his hands. The snow swirled aggressively around them. They both seemed to notice the thickness of it and the dark weighing on them. Tony stared blankly into the snow. Beck grabbed his elbow and tried to urge them to keep moving. They needed to keep moving.

"Tony, come on."

"Who would have tried to kill her?"

Beck paused, he had a feeling that it wasn't just Susanna who was targeted.

"The three of you were in the car, right?" Beck asked.

"Yes."

"So maybe it was someone who was coming for all three of you?"

A knot formed in the pit of Tony's stomach and wrenched itself around. He turned away from Beck and puked, which made a hole in the snow about two feet down. Tony and Beck walked in silence the rest of the way back toward the house. They were positive they had been walking for over an hour, but in front of them there was nothing but empty darkness and whipping blankets of blowing snow. At this point they could hardly move and were only comforted by the fact that they were together. Had they been alone they were sure they would have been dead. Tony and Beck stopped and looked at each other. They were too cold to speak, but they knew what one another was thinking. Tony started to kneel toward the ground, and Beck reached under his arms and pulled him back up.

"I need some sleep, then we'll keep moving."

"Nope, you're staying up. Please."

"It's okay."

"No, no, it's not okay." Beck's voice was wavering. Now, he was afraid that they weren't going to make it. If Tony gave up now, how was he supposed to carry on? He looked out into the endless darkness. They had been following the road so there were still street lights every hundred metres or so.

"I'm sure we don't have much further to go. Come on." Beck wrapped Tony's arm around his shoulder and began trudging along in the snow. Beck's eyes were filled with tears now, which began to freeze as they fell and curled under his jaw. He was so angry at Tony, but he wasn't about to lose him. He was surprised at how little Tony weighed now. He hadn't noticed. Beck almost thought he could carry his thin body. He felt Tony's troubled heart beating against his own. Even someone who was supposed to lead, supposed to know it all, struggled to make decisions as tough as this one. Tony lost his daughter through trying to protect her and save her. Beck thought about himself. Tony couldn't save him, but still chose to keep him close.

Tony muttered something but Beck didn't hear what it was through the blowing of the snow and deafening cold in the wind.

"What did you say?" Beck's voice was hardly audible it was shaking so much.

"I'm sorry."

"No, no, we're not doing that."

"That's not your call, kid."

Beck smiled. This sounded more like Tony. Tony started to sink into Beck's arms, and Beck realized he was taking almost all of his weight.

"You've got to stay up, sir."

The two of them buckled into the snow and Beck's torso to his knees sank into the infinite white. He pulled Tony's upper half into his arms and laid him against his chest.

"Hey, stay awake, please," Beck pleaded. Tony didn't answer. Beck's vision was blurred by the snow and his frozen tears weighed on his face. He didn't know what he was seeing now as he strained to look out into the road. He was holding onto Tony so tightly, as if he were able to transfer his warmth and life into him. Two street lights seemed to converge in the distance, and Beck thought he was hallucinating now. He put his head down and hugged Tony closer to him. He was still breathing but at a very slow pace. Beck saw the insides of his eyelids turn a bright orange, and opened them to see a car speeding along the road toward them. Beck waved his arms up and down frantically, and the car half pulled over, half slid to a stop beside them. Beck strained again to see. It was his own car, and he looked up to see Paul running around the side of it toward them. He knelt down and picked up Tony's frail body in one swing, and put him in the back seat, covering him with blankets already in the back of the car. He returned and helped Beck up, wrapping him in another blanket. Beck hugged him without even thinking. Never had he been so happy to see someone. Paul smiled and hugged him back. He helped him into the front seat and tilted it so he could fall asleep. Beck was out cold before Paul had gotten into the driver's seat and turned around to head home. His mind throbbed with a slowly thawing icy headache.

#

Beck woke up on the emerald-green couch of Tony and Paul's living room. He rolled over and fell to the floor with a thud. He sat up gingerly, groaning as he took in the smell of wet dog, realizing that it was steaming off of his own body.

"Everything all right in there?" Beck heard Paul's familiar accent. Beck sat up and placed his elbows on his knees and his head in his hands. His head was still throbbing from the cold, the stress, the alcohol, and the ache of being kept in the dark.

"What happened?" Beck muttered. Paul had come into the living room and held out toast with raspberry jam and a glass of orange juice. Beck smiled and took it from him.

"Well, from what I've gathered, you two were quite angry with one another, whether it was warranted or not is not my place to say, but you ended up at the bar down the road, and then it started bloody snowing. The car wouldn't start so you began walking back and you were drunk so you weren't really sure how much time had passed. Tony's sick anyway, so then it was downhill from there. I started getting worried so I came to find you."

"Wow, yes, that sounds about right. My version is much less clear. Thanks for the food."

"You're welcome."

"What do you mean Tony's sick?"

"Oh, I assumed he'd told you with everything else."

"No, he definitely didn't."

"He's got cancer, Beck."

"What?" Beck's stomach felt as though it were turning in a meat grinder. He placed his toast and juice on the coffee table in front of him and spoke slowly. "Cancer?" He was hardly able to mutter the word. Of everything Tony had left until now to tell him, this was the hardest blow.

"Well, he had kidney cancer, presumably from drinking, but he beat it a while ago so we thought he was in the clear. About a month ago it was back and it had spread." Paul's voice was somber, though his words almost sounded rehearsed. Beck wondered if he'd practised what he would have to tell everyone when he lost his best friend.

"Can I talk to him?"

"He's asleep. He's all right now, don't worry. I want you to eat, please." Beck nodded. Paul looked worried. Beck wondered how much Paul knew, and momentarily felt worried and sad himself. Someone who quietly did so much for both Tony and Beck without arguing would soon be alone without either of them. Beck climbed back up on the couch and wrapped himself in the blanket. It smelled like home, whatever that meant, but it prompted an urge to call Mary and the boys. Paul had started back toward the kitchen.

"Paul?"

Paul turned around. "Yes?"

"Could I use the phone?"

"Absolutely, but I'm not sure how well it'll work given the storm last night."

Beck stood, the blanket still wrapped around him and sauntered over to the phone on the wall by the fireplace. The embers from the night before were still hot. Paul must have started a fire to keep him warm.

Beck dialed the number to his aunt's house slowly. He was unsure what he was going to tell her. He was unsure what he should tell her. He was unsure what he was allowed to tell her.

The phone rang a few times before he heard a familiar raspy voice on the other end.

"Hello?"

"Hi, Mary."

Beck could feel Mary's smile through the phone. "Oh Beck, it's so nice to hear from you, honey. You know you've got to call me more often, love."

"I know, Mary, I'm so sorry. I've been busy."

"I know. But we're all busy, hon." Beck felt her hurt, even if she responded in an understanding tone. He paused for a moment, realizing he didn't have words to say. Beck had always loved Mary. She had raised him and loved him and welcomed him with everything she had, despite being a single mother with two other children. He felt immense guilt for how independent and reserved he had been in his late childhood and teenage years. He went off on his own and didn't ever tell Mary how much she meant to him.

"I just wanted to call and check in," Beck finally replied.

"Oh, well, thank you. We're doing well. How is your new job going?"

"It's going great, actually, I've made some wonderful friends." Beck felt his voice crack with the tears in his throat and hoped it wasn't noticeable over the phone. He swallowed them once he finished his sentence. Beck's back was turned to the hallway that led to the bedrooms, but Tony had come out of his room and leaned against the door, listening. He too had tears in his eyes.

"That's wonderful, Beck, I'm so happy for you. We are all really proud of you back here. Will you be coming by for Christmas?"

Beck felt the tears collecting deep in the back of his throat now. He didn't know how to answer. He really wasn't sure. With all his heart he wanted to wrap Mary in his arms — her small little self with once beautiful bouncy curls, now streaked with stress-ridden tones of grey. In his eyes she was still beautiful, and she reminded him so much of his mother. She was the last bit of his family he had left.

"I'll be there. I promise." Beck knew instantly that he'd made a promise he wouldn't keep.

"Wonderful! I'll do the stuffing the way you like it, then. They boys won't eat it, but I know you love it." Beck's eyes clouded over with warm salty water, as he soaked in Mary's excitement on the other end of the phone.

"Thank you. I'm looking forward to it. So much."

"Are you sure everything's okay, honey? You sound a little funny."

"Oh I'm just a little sick. The weather's been dreadful here."

"I heard about that snowstorm coming through! I hope you kept warm last night!"

"I was. I actually stayed at a friend's house." Beck smiled, shaking his head at the night before.

Tony smiled at the ground and shuffled his feet. Beck turned around and saw him standing in the hall.

"That's nice. It warms my heart that you've made good friends," Mary replied, but Beck only half heard her. He was so happy to see Tony standing across from him, smiling.

"Yeah, I've got to go, but I'll talk to you soon," Beck answered.

"Okay, hon, I love you, you know that?" Beck felt a sharp pain in his chest as both fear and bravery began to take shape together.

"I know, I love you too, Mary." Beck hung up the phone. He turned back to Tony, who was still leaning against the doorway. His hands were in his pockets. Once Beck turned around he took them out.

"You're awake?" Beck tried to sound put together.

"So are you."

"Well I never blacked out. Clearly I hold my alcohol better."

"That might be pushing it." Tony smiled. They paused for a second, holding eye contact. Beck ran to him and hugged him, which Tony didn't realize he'd hoped he would do.

"This is quite the emotional roller coaster, huh?" Tony said, his hands cupping Beck's head to his chest.

"You could say that," Beck replied, trying desperately not to cry. "But it's your fault."

Tony nodded. "Fair." When they pulled away it was almost as if someone had flipped a switch for their emotional states.

"We've got a lot to do today." Tony stretched his arms up in the air and made windmill circles with them.

"I think you should be sleeping today."

"Sleep is for the weak, Mr. Brooks."

"Not when you've got cancer, sir."

Tony looked at Beck sternly. "Paul?" he shouted to the kitchen.

Paul came around the corner, a partially eaten piece of toast in hand. "Yes, your highness?"

"Oh quit it," Tony replied somewhat angrily. "You told him? I thought I said don't tell the kid?"

"Tony, he deserved to know after everything else you've hidden from him. Not that I'm surprised."

"Surprised?"

"You hide nearly everything from me too." Paul's patient voice was irritatingly calm to Tony. They looked hard at one another. Neither of them wanted to reopen the scabs of their past right now. Tony looked at the floor first.

"A thank you would be, you know, nice," Paul said quietly before walking back into the kitchen.

"Um," Beck tried to break the silence.

"Is that your toast?" Tony interrupted.

"Yes."

"You want it?"

"No, not really."

Tony bent down and took a massive bite out of it and downed the orange juice, which Beck did actually want.

"Give me five minutes and we're going downstairs to talk more."

"I think you need to rest."

"I don't need you telling me what *you* think I should do, Brooks. I'm time limited and so are you. Downstairs in five, please." Beck didn't argue. Before, he had only ever felt the authority and power in Tony's voice. Now, he sensed every bit of panic and worry. He needed more answers.

"Her memory links are fading, Becker. You need to go back in."

"What?" Beck thought his heart stopped beating.

"Downstairs. Five minutes."

#

Beck was sitting on one of the stools waiting patiently when Tony came cautiously down the stairs. It was obvious that he was in pain.

"Here's what we're doing. I'm going to stay here and figure out what we need to do. You're going to see Penny. It's one of the more important links. Last night when I checked, it was fading which means someone has beaten us to her. You need to find her, you hear me?"

"I'm on it. Can I ask something quickly?"

"Sure."

"All these important memories are simple. They feel like everyday things. How are they so important?"

"Great question. Maybe that's intentional. Maybe this is what God or the universe likes about her so much."

Beck nodded. It's what he liked about her. He climbed into the APM without much argument now, and Tony closed the lid.

\#

When Beck woke up he found himself in the middle of a bike path beside a perfectly manicured lawn, and across from an array of castle-like buildings. *Oh so she went to Oxford, of course*, Beck thought.

"Tony, you could have been more specific with this."

"Give me a second, I'm finding her. She's in the hall across from you, about to walk out. Go ask her out or something."

"Oh so now I'm allowed to do that?"

"I'm leaving. I'll come back on comms when I get back. You're on your own for right now."

"Got it." Beck reached up and turned off his earpiece. He saw Penny emerge from the towering building and took a deep breath before jogging across the grass to her. No matter how many times he'd done this, he still got nervous. But he'd already been in her younger memories. She should know him here. Beck tapped her on the shoulder but she didn't turn around.

"Can I help you?"

Beck smiled. Always the same response. "Maybe."

"Not interested."

"Yes, actually you are. I need you to come with me."

Penny paused for a second. His voice sounded familiar. She spun around.

"Beck." A soft smile found its way into her cheeks.

Beck smiled at her. He could tell she was happy to see him, but they didn't have time.

"We've got to go, just trust me." He took her hands in his, and uncharacteristically she didn't resist. "There are people after you here." He thought that he might have been a bit aggressive given there was no imminent threat that Beck could see.

"Okay," she said, searching his eyes. It was weird how blindly she'd learned to trust him. In her pocket, she wrapped her hand around the small piece of paper that she'd had in her memories since she was a child. She carried it with her everywhere. In real life, as these memories with Beck appeared, she'd accepted them there, knowing one day she'd have answers. She felt she hadn't lived them, which she hadn't, though her essence had. They'd never actually met, which Penny always found fascinating, but she trusted the fact that she felt love without having lived it.

"When will we really meet?"

"1979, promise."

Beck took her hand and they started walking. "We need to keep a low profile. Anywhere we could go?"

"Well there's usually a lot of people on the main street. We could blend in."

"All right, let's go."

They walked for a few minutes. Beck looked around noticing the clarity of everything. Penny's attention to detail was unparalleled. He noticed now how well he could smell everything too — the small bakery, gasoline, and the freshly cut lawn. He watched her for a moment, her eyes darting about, absorbing everything. In the corner of his eye, he thought he saw someone. Four men in dark suits were running toward them.

"Penny, get on my back," Beck said sternly.

"I'm perfectly fine to walk, thank you." She looked at him, horrified at the thought of being piggy-backed.

"Penny! We need to run and you can't run!"

Beck scooped her up like a child and took off, darting around the people on the street.

"Why is no one reacting to anything?" Penny yelled.

"Because these are just your memories, they aren't real, remember? Just a construction of what you remember from this day and time."

"They're getting closer!"

One man pulled a gun from his pocket. Beck darted behind a group of people as he heard it fire. They shimmied into a small comic book store and hid behind a tall shelf, gasping for air.

"You read any of this?" Beck whispered, trying to ease the tension. He looked down at her, realizing she was still tucked into his arms and holding onto him tightly.

"No, do you?" She looked up to meet his eyes. He noticed she didn't shift her weight, and their proximity didn't change.

"I did around now. What year is it?"

"1969."

"I was a teenager about now, so, yeah."

"That's cute," she whispered.

A book fell from the shelf and Beck clasped his hand around Penny's mouth. Thick boots collided with each step against the tile floor, but Penny and Beck could tell the pursuer was trying to be quiet. Some other people entered now. Beck peered around the corner and saw what looked like FBI agents. He sat back, his sweat dripping down his forehead and his hands tightening around Penny. They weren't just trying to change her memories. That would have been easy. Tony had said Beck could do it simply by interacting with her. This was different. They were trying to kill her. What happens if you die in your memories? Beck gulped down his fear and confusion.

A bullet shot through the bookshelf in front of them and hit the wall above their heads. Through it, one of the men in the black suits was staring at them through his masked face and began to walk over. He stopped in front of them, the gun pointed at Penny. They both stood and Beck leapt in front of her.

"What the hell do you want?" Beck asked coldly.

"I want her to pay for what she's done to me."

"To you?" Beck was confused. He had been told the government Sifters were after them. Sifters were more or less assassins with no personal agenda. For the most part, their job and who they target doesn't mean anything to them. This guy knew Penny.

"Who are you?" Penny said, peeking her head out from behind Beck. All you could see through the man's face mask were his eyes, which looked eerily familiar. The man held the gun pointed at them, but his hand shook tremendously.

"If you want to shoot her you're going to have to shoot me too."

"You're the last person I want to shoot." The man's accent was unmistakable.

"Go," he said suddenly, "before the others get here."

Penny and Beck were alarmed. One minute they were held at gunpoint and another they were being protected. The two of them shimmied through the comic book shop, dodging between splintered shelves, watching the man sit down and hold his head in his hands. Beck and Penny headed down the street, trying to blend in as much as possible. They needed to find a safe place.

Once they found a small park, densely populated with trees, they sat underneath one in the grass to catch their breath.

"Do you have any idea who that was?" Penny asked Beck, who was clearly out of breath.

"Not a clue," he lied. "Could have been anyone." Beck leaned back against the cool bark of the tree. He needed to ask Tony some things and was making a mental note in his head.

"You're lying. You know it couldn't have been."

"What?" She'd caught Beck off guard.

"It was Paul Elliott."

#

"Tony, they aren't just trying to change her memories, they are trying to kill her in them."

"Yeah, I figured that might happen."

"Why? Why kill her?"

"They know what's going on. But if you die in your memory, then that part of the essence's connection with its future is completely severed. They are eliminating the chance that they only weaken it. The connection wouldn't exist anymore."

"But wouldn't she die in real life?"

"No, she'd just lose that memory. They are just her memories, remember. Not actually the past."

"Do they know where her essence is going?"

"I'd imagine so."

"Why are they so concerned about her?"

"There's much more about this we have yet to figure out, and I won't be able to figure it out in my lifetime. That's up to you and Penny. But we can't control or predict why things happen. There has to be a way to unlock all the memories of the past that have collected inside each of us. This migration of essences is not genetic, though it's generational. They are passed on at random and dispersed across the world. There could be an essence in Africa going to one in Spain. The more the government shits around with it, the more random it gets. If you're asking me, I think the big man upstairs has had it. Penny is a reset."

"So if there is a God, he's trying to fix this mess we've made."

"Yes, and He's trusted all of us."

"Do you think the government knows how to access the memories of the past as they're passed on?"

Tony paused a moment, considering what Beck had said. He looked up at the white speckled ceiling. There had to be billions of little plaster speckles, all just for viewing pleasure.

"I don't know. But if they do, I don't expect they've been diligent about including it in the history books."

"It makes you wonder, doesn't it?"

"What?"

"Whose memories Penny has, besides her own." Beck paused. He was nervous about bringing up this next part. "There's something else. There was a Sifter in there, who knew us."

"What do you mean?" Tony sounded concerned.

"He really knew us."

"I don't understand."

"Didn't you say Sifters have no agenda? No personal stake?"

Tony sat down. "They're brainwashed. They don't actually have any agency. They don't know what they're doing."

"Well, this one did. He said he wanted to make Penny pay for what she did. He sounded like Paul."

The phone rang upstairs.

Beck gulped. He knew who it was. "Let me get it!"

#

With each day that passed in December of 1979, Penny's mind was intruded, captivated, and pelted with unfamiliar emotive memories. She was confused, so she sat still, trying to write. A source of electric light burst in during the most ordinary days in the dimly lit, streetside coffee shops. She felt love for someone she had never met, alongside powerful, lengthy, and ever growing memories. At first, she didn't think anything of it. She thought her writing had inspired a memory, and thought of her friend in college, Gabby, who had once shown her a photo of Becker Brooks. The kid whose parents had died. Penny remembered him vividly. As memories with him spontaneously surfaced in her mind, she felt as though she'd missed something, though she gained it. She felt as though she were revisiting memories, realizing that she wasn't the only one there. Water, she had read, carried its past, forever seeking where it was. It moves between us and through us. It is as much multigenerational as it is intragenerational. Its fluidity, composing most of our bodies, guides us in memories that are not our own. Penny thought in storytelling. But here she was, rapidly more unsure. *Do I tell yours or mine?* They were, one could say linked, but as rapidly as they had intertwined in her memories, they could be unwound. *Hurry,* something told her.

As Penny sat in her usual spot in a coffee shop, late at night, memories poured into her. It seemed to flow like the state she found herself in when she wrote, transcribing fiction from theatres hosting stage shows in her mind. Winnie often pushed her to differentiate between knowledge and God's wisdom, which Penny never quite understood or thought anything of until now. *We choose which voices we listen to, but the voices are always there*, Winnie had said. Penny stood and followed a memory that she did not recognize, packing her belongings and leaving her coffee. She realized she knew things she hadn't known before now, despite not having moved from her spot for two hours. These new memories didn't startle her, but what did startle her was the intuition when it came. She needed to find Tony and Paul because Becker Brooks had told her to years earlier, and she only remembered it now. They'd never met, had they? She needed to find all three of them.

"Excuse me," her voice shook, "could I use the phone?"

Gently, the radio on the counter tried to pour out Bob Dylan's warning medicine. The times were truly about to change. Penny picked up the receiver. Her hands were shaking as she dialed. She couldn't remember the number. She dug into her brain, finding three perfect squares and a small piece of paper that existed only as a memory. Her fingers pressed buttons. *609-144-2550*. The phone rang on the other end, baring the shrill noise of uncertainty. Becker Brooks sent her mind spinning. There were a series of moments in her mind, expecting loyalty to a truth neither of them wrote. She was drawn to him, but not because he was her prince, or because he carried a particular label.

"Hello?" a familiar voice answered. Penny gasped in air that went down the wrong way, causing a pain in her chest.

"Beck?"

"Pen, thank God."

CHAPTER 13

– Love –

December 1979, Kingston, New Jersey

Paul had always been the quieter, more introspective of the pair. He was equally as brilliant as Tony, just without the charisma, wit, and personality of the front of a magazine. He didn't always agree with the tenacity that founded Tony's actions, but he couldn't be without him. He often chose to say nothing, or agreed to disagree. His parents had both fled a war-torn England as children. His father grew up craving a better life and through his passions in medicine, he studied to become a doctor. His only setback was the rapidly approaching second war and the sweeping romance he tumbled into with Paul's mother, who was a poet, poor, and tensed Mr. Elliott's heart and singular trust in science. Paul loved his parents more than anything in the world. He admired their courage and brave pursuit of happiness and peace in the midst of some of the most troubling forty years the world had seen. But he didn't understand what the war had done to them external to his interactions with their kindness and love of learning.

He hadn't kept much from the old house in the Bronx. Tony felt like home in a way the house never did. But Paul had kept a box, filled mostly with the remnants of his parent's lives — a few photographs and handwritten notes to one another. Paul opened it when he missed Susanna or Penny, wrestling with the interception of love and the work he did. Sometimes he opened it when he needed to read the words passed between his parents — words that likewise described how much he loved his best friend. They were words he couldn't speak out loud.

In December 1979, Paul sat with this box while Tony worked with Beck in the basement, the day after the bar incident. The house still smelled like its old inhabitants. Paul liked that Tony liked it — he often noted, truthfully, that it reminded them that someone had always walked through and lived in a place before them. Paul sat on the edge of his bed, thumbing through the photographs and letters. He could hear Tony's foot tapping beneath him and was sure his mind was doing the same thing. As Paul went to replace the lid of the box, a small compartment in it fell open. Two birth certificates slid out. Paul felt his heart valves squeeze as he unrolled them. One was his, and one read: Mark Jones Elliott. Paul squinted to see the birth date and felt his throat close.

As a child, he didn't remember a time when work wasn't scarce. He was hungry often and his parents' eyes had always been dark. He remembered that their smiles only emerged from the shadows of soot on their faces when he prompted them. Paul's father had sat him down to talk about the meaning of what was happening in 1930's New York, and across all of America. Mr. Elliott spoke of immense loss, leaving perhaps the most crucial piece of this truth as searing pain behind his eyes and in the lines of his face. The dampening of life continued to weave its way through neighbourhoods, communities, cities, and states. Paul had a hard time not noticing his parent's demeanour, their fatigue and their wretched bodies stumbling into the house at the end of the day. But he never thought that there might have been another catalyst — one who had lived. Paul crunched the certificate in his hand, grabbed his keys and headed to the car. He smoothed it out against his thigh as he drove along the grainy wet roads.

#

"Paul, what are you doing here? You could be arrested."

Paul said nothing, placing the certificate down on Mark's desk.

"What is this?"

"Read it."

The colour evaporated from Mark's face. "Where did you find this, Paul?"

"Did you know?"

"Where did you find it?"

Paul gritted his teeth, fighting the anger seeping into his voice. "Did you know?" he asked sternly.

Mark breathed deeply, closing his eyes, and gripping his desk, the certificate still in his hand. "Yes, Paul, I knew. They left me in an orphanage when I was ten, and then it burned down like everything else."

"Why?"

"They were young. They had no money. So I figured it out."

Paul was quiet. He didn't know what to say. He felt hurt because Mark had been hurt. He felt frustrated because he didn't understand. He felt conflicted by compassion and anger as he thought about the choices his brother had made. It had been Mark all this time.

"Why?"

"Why what?"

"Why are you doing this, then?"

"Because it hurts you."

Paul nodded at the floor, putting his hands on his hips. "That doesn't add up, Mark. If you want to hurt me, why hurt all these people?"

"I hated you. I hated looking in those windows seeing you grow up with your soulmate best friend and *my* parents who loved *you*. It was a story I didn't get the chance to live and a memory I didn't get the chance to make. So I tracked you down, got in where I needed to, and now I've got this whole project operating for me."

"So you're hoarding them now? All those people's memories and stories. You can't even access them."

Mark's glare turned sinister. He smiled and shook his head. "What do you think I do here all day? Spend my life making sure you're doing your job? I know you're not. You two never have. Once I saw what you were doing, twenty-five years ago, I started working too. Turns out Susanna was much more than a pretty face."

"Most women are. What do you mean?"

"She had this figured out in the '50s and you two had her shunned away in Salem with this mind of gold. She had more answers in a few years of research than you and Crypt have had in your entire life. She knew its potential, so she buried it. Infantile Amnesia turned out to be the key. I tried to forget the good memories I had with our parents. I wanted them out of my head. Susanna tapped into the fact that memories are only forgotten before the age of four. Do you know why?"

Paul shook his head no. Susanna hardly told them anything she was doing on her end, minus the small tasks she did when she wasn't taking care of Penny. Now, he saw why she kept quiet and so distant.

Paul had backed against the wall as Mark walked around the front of his desk. He'd always been afraid of him, but now he was terrified.

Mark's explanation was frantically energized and Paul almost missed pieces of it. "Our brains start making more complicated, useful connections through neurogenesis. From birth to age four, our minds are almost photographic. They remember everything, and the hippocampus is working overtime. As we no longer need our earliest memories, they are detached from their ability to reach our consciousness and reconnected to orchestrate a space for something else to live — our personal library of essences from the past. The connections between this set of memories and our own is heightened in sleep, as the hippocampus stores our most vivid experiences, and stirs up our deepest memories."

"I don't understand, how do you access it?"

"It's a bit like a cloud, deep in the hippocampus, in a place we've never thought to look. Once activated, well, the rest is easy."

"What, what, what..."

"What made me look? Rather, what made me go looking deep in Susanna's work files?" Mark laughed hysterically, filling the room with insidious echoes.

"I needed to get to all three of you. I needed your work and your help so I took away the one person who was holding you and Tony together. Then I turned her house upside down. It took me years of sneaking onto that property. I wanted to know what she knew or what you two had possibly hidden there. It's funny isn't it — you didn't even know something was hidden! I also wanted to know where her essence went. And it wasn't much of a shock to find out that you've now acquired him too. It is disgusting how much the universe is fighting against me."

"Beck." Paul stumbled, hardly able to mutter the words. He had known this, but his mind was racing. What had they done.

"I was desperate to deprive you, but that essence was bloody determined to get back to you. So what was I left with?"

Paul was frozen in place. His heart felt pain, not anger. Mark's actions drew him into a seeping guilt that he had to try and unravel.

"Mark, revenge won't give you love that somebody else had or has. It won't give you what you didn't have in the past." Paul's voice was soft but shaking. He had been subtly searching the room. *Show me something, Susy.* On Mark's desk, there was a red leather book.

"Oh, I think it will. You two never did stumble across how to unlock all these memories once they're passed on. You know they're there, in the brain, but you can't get to them. Seems I can now, thanks to Susanna. Clearly she never intended to help you figure it out. It turns out, if I redirect what essences I want to wherever my essence is headed next, I can do exactly what you say I can't. It wasn't hard to brainwash all of those Sifters using some old war tactics. It's hilarious! They haven't the slightest idea what they're doing!"

"They're not your memories, Mark."

"No, but then again, aren't we all a by-product of our past? Epigenetics, nature, nurture?"

"That's not what this is about."

"Then what's it about, Paul?" Mark was mocking. Paul stared. All these years he had hated Mark. He thought of him simply as the next asshole in a long line of supremacist, egotistical capitalists. Tony and Paul had been quick to blame the government. And maybe they were partially to blame. People followed Mark, assuming his actions were rooted in the Sifting Project's original purpose. This whole time, Mark had been composing horror. The work that Paul and Tony had been doing was now infinitely more complicated. Paul's mind was saturated with the past twenty minutes and chipped pieces of his heart. He couldn't understand the apathetic rage that forced someone into these actions for twenty-five years. His brother.

Paul thought of Tony in this moment. Paul *could* understand. He took a deep breath.

"It's about empathy, Mark. It's about allowing people's memories to just be in their truth. People live different lives, all over the world. They make different choices. There are good and bad memories, stories and experiences that we now carry. We have to carry them with compassion. We have to give them all a chance to teach us. We have to give them a chance to just exist. We can't hoard them or redistribute them or decide when and if they're useful to us."

"You sound like Tony."

"No. I sound like we all should sound."

"The people being sifted don't even know what's happening. They'll never know."

"We don't know that. You just said so yourself. Think about dreams, nightmares, déjà vu."

Mark laughed, shaking his head. "You're naive. This is capitalism. We capitalize on people too. If their memories tell too much of the truth it ruins us."

"How? Because you benefit from their oppression? That's what you've been taught. And it's dangerous to think that way. But that doesn't make you the problem. You have an experience that is valid too, and tortured, and I'm sorry. But it will collect in your essence, and it will go where it is needed next. If you say you can access past essences, collected within people, wouldn't you want the person down the line from you to be able to see your story? Your past can teach you. The essences in you can teach you. But they are not who you are. You cannot turn the joys preserved in someone else's memories into your own. You can see them, love them, appreciate them, and lift them up. They may help you create your own joy but they aren't yours. They stand up in their own right." Paul started walking toward the desk.

"How are you like this? I killed her, Paul. I killed her!"

"Because I believe there's always a reason for people's actions. Living with Tony will teach you that."

"Get out." Mark turned away, looking out the window into the busy street. Paul grabbed the red notebook and slid it into his jacket.

"Mark, please. Help us. Don't be a victim of the memories you've been taught to hold on to. We can free the past, including yours."

"Get out."

#

As Paul drove back to the house, he tried to piece things together enough to heal before walking through the front door. His face grew hot and his hair damp as memories of mistakes whipped around the trunks of confusion, anger, and love that Tony had undoubtedly planted throughout their lives. Paul didn't know what to do now. Tony was this ball of sarcastic humour and energy that made him feel alive. Paul felt more confident and assertive around him. Tony made him feel like he could do anything. Paul knew that something in Tony had changed in their early teenage years and he thought he was the only one to notice. The energetic boy became cynical and often turned inward and alone. Paul felt himself a nuisance to Tony — someone he had never feared. The two boys believed in their ability to solve any problem that came their way except the one between them. When it came to friendship, loyalty, trust, and consistency, Tony was unsure of himself, and Paul was unsure of Tony's uncertainty. But they were able to drug it with love — the elephant in the room. They were always motivated by passion.

As they had matured, Paul became jealous of Tony's ability to intoxicate people. He seemed to be able to collect all possible surface-level relationships, and avoid the only one that mattered. Paul only wanted to be Tony's confidante — he didn't want to live in his shadow. Still, they did everything together. Even in silence they were each other's greatest comfort during the long nights alone in the drafty house, like every other along their lonely street. Tony idolized Paul's calmness and genuine heart. He believed that Paul kept him sane despite the fear with which his mind operated. Because they never spoke of the meaning of their friendship, they were always unsure. They thought of themselves as meaningless in the eyes of the other when the opposite was true. When the day came and their parents left for war, Paul knew some of the good in his heart had turned inward. He'd felt neglected, taken advantage of, and utterly alone. In the days after their parents left, they ate, cleaned, and did tasks out of bare necessity without speaking a single word. Paul could see that day vividly now, as if he were driving toward it, unable to brake. He had sat in his corner of the room, his silence even more prevalent than it usually was. When Tony walked in, he sat on the corner of Paul's mattress, which was on the same wall as his own. They both liked looking out the window when they woke up.

"Paul, I don't know what to say."

"That's because you have nothing to say to me. Don't talk to me."

Paul had felt many unfamiliar emotions swirling in his throat, many of which he felt now, but under it all he sensed why Tony did what he did. Tony was afraid of being alone. He was afraid of life without Paul. Though it burned with acidity, Paul knew that he was afraid of the same thing. As much as they had grown apart in their own ways, they had a bond that was unbreakable like the soul of a God in the hands of Hades. Although, the strength that illuminated the fibre of the thread would struggle to be as bright as it once had been.

Memories continued to flood Paul's consciousness, saturating his mind with a different emotion each time. Many were memories he forgot he had because he had tried to shut them out. Susanna had painted him. All at once he remembered how hard he'd tried not to love her.

He was right back with her, sitting at the picnic tables outside their afternoon biophysics class decades ago. Paul loved that she was one of only two girls in the class. They often met here for lunch between their morning and afternoon classes. It was something they never told Tony about because it allowed them to be alone. It allowed both of them to think away from Tony, whose passion was often overpowering. The three of them didn't understand what the scope of their relationships with each other was. It was a complicated love that you couldn't put a label on. So they didn't.

"What exactly happened between you two anyway?"

"What do you mean?" Paul took a huge first bite out of his crunchy peanut butter sandwich. He always put too much on it, Susanna thought, watching the buttery oil ooze out the sides of his pumpernickel bread.

"I mean," she paused to hand him a napkin as he clumsily wiped his face and laughed, "how are you two so close, but also so damn tense all the time?"

Paul paused, using the fact that he was chewing to allow him to think. He wasn't sure how to respond. Love was a painful thing sometimes.

"I suppose I'll always be angry at him, but I don't care about him any less."

"That's a good way to put it. But won't you tell me why?" She tucked a thick red curl behind her ear, which meant she was listening intently. She was one of the rare few who looked people in the eyes when they spoke. This was what made her so attractive in Paul's opinion. She was a wonderful listener because she listened to listen, not respond. This was something Paul congruently hated about Tony. His attention span was the length of a fingernail. Paul stared at Susanna for a moment. She captivated many eyes until they saw her passion for academia. People didn't quite approve of that either, but Paul didn't care, wondering why he seemed to defy the affinity. He just wanted her presence in his life. When he would eventually give it up, it would grate his heart to shreds.

"Don't worry about our issues, they are long in the past."

"I beg to differ." She rested her chin on her hands on the table, looking up into his eyes.

"Tony did something horrible when we were really young teenagers. I will never forgive him for it. But he's my best friend and I need him in my life. I wish he would grow up sometime soon, but I don't ever want to lose him." He was surprised by how easily these words fell out of his mouth to Susanna.

"Okay," she responded, "that's fair." Though it was evident that she wasn't content with his response. "If you hold onto that too long it will kill you, you know."

"What?"

"You have to let it run its course. That's how we forgive."

Paul smiled. "What if I can't?"

"That part is up to you, isn't it?"

Paul's gaze softened. "You really are just Lady Wisdom, huh?"

"I try." She smiled. "We should go to class, you know."

"Do we need to? Can't you teach me everything we're going to learn?"

"Ah, physics is different. You have to pay attention."

"And you can become wise without paying attention?"

"Touché." She stood to pack her books. "I'll see you later?"

Paul rolled his eyes and smiled back. "Hard to get, that's fine."

"The hardest to get." She winked.

"I'm not in a rush," Paul called after her. He sounded more self-assured than he ever had.

Paul's mind now pushed further. He gripped the steering wheel as if he could suffocate it out of his thoughts. Another memory swelled and began to take shape. Perhaps the most painful yet, in 1950.

"You know, I hate that you can't work," Paul said one morning before he walked out the door.

"*You* hate it?" Susanna hugged Penny who was sitting on her lap, trying to braid her hair.

"You're right, I know. I can't imagine."

"I made a choice. It keeps her safe."

"My fingers are stuck in your hair, Mommy," Penny replied. Susanna smiled brightly at her, untangling her small fingers. Susanna was constantly worried about Penny's dark hair. It biologically wasn't possible given that Susanna and Paul both had red hair. Tony was aware of this too, which drew him threateningly close to Penny.

"Do you want to go to the lab today?" Paul asked her.

"I don't know how I feel about sneaking into a government building anymore. It's really not right. We've talked about this. The work is exhilarating, but it's wrong."

"Susy, nobody knows anything," Tony called from the kitchen. His voice sounded much louder in the confines of their small shared apartment. "I'd feel more wrong going behind Satan's back."

"You can't just quit, we need you," Paul added calmly.

"That's not what I mean."

"That's what this is about?"

"We have a very young child, Paul, the last thing I want is to put her in danger. Research like this has a cost. It's dangerous because you're passionate, not curious."

"This is your life's work, Susanna. Don't give up on it because of..."

"Because of what, Paul?" Susanna's tone had changed, which startled him. "Because of the kid you didn't intend to have? Because I love both of you? Because I value those things over going behind the government's back for research we should probably leave alone?"

"I didn't say that." Paul was calm in his response, but shocked by Susanna's words and anger.

"No, of course not. You know, you're really quick to conspire. The corruption in science isn't science's fault. The problem is that it's the only thing you trust. It's not going to give you all the answers."

"Susanna, what the hell?" Paul matched her tone now.

"This is more your child than Penny is! You never come home to her, Paul! Or me!"

"I come home," Tony added obnoxiously from the kitchen.

"Shut up, Tony. This doesn't involve you right now."

"Oh, I think it does," Tony replied sternly, entering the room now.

Susanna shot daggers in Tony's direction and he matched her gaze. She knew exactly what he was referring to, and she refused to tell Paul. She would never tell him. No matter what path he chose.

"I can't do this anymore." Susanna stood, carrying Penny. "We're leaving."

"And where exactly are you going?" Paul asked angrily.

"My mother's house in Salem. Tomorrow morning. I want to keep her safe."

"I never said I didn't."

"Well if you do, then I think this should end, between us three."

"Susanna."

Susanna walked to Penny's room and told her to stay and play. She came back and sat on the edge of the couch and put her head in her hands. Paul walked over and sat beside her. He slowly wrapped his arms around her, and she let him, as soft, painful tears absorbed into his chest.

"We'll figure this out," Paul tried to assure her, but there was unease in his voice.

"I'm afraid for her, Paul. I'm sure they know something by now."

"Go to Salem, we'll visit every chance we can." Paul looked up at Tony who nodded in agreement.

"I don't think you should. I don't want to give anyone another chance to find us."

"You're being a little paranoid, don't you think?" Tony added.

"Tony, fuck off!"

"Hey, hey, hey." Paul pulled her head into his chest. "It's not his kid, he doesn't understand."

"Oh, I understand perfectly," Tony said, staring directly at Susanna. She didn't look up.

"What do you want, Tony?" Paul asked, annoyed.

"I'm just a very truthful person."

"Would you just give us some space, please? Not everything is about you."

"Gladly." Tony grabbed his keys off the counter and stormed out the front door, more willingly than Paul thought he would.

"Susanna, I'm not going to let you walk out of my life," Paul said calmly, stroking her hair and tucking it behind her ear.

"Well then you decide what's more important. Us, or him."

"It's not a matter of that."

"I think it is, Paul."

"I'm passionate about my work."

"That's your problem. You know you take a back seat to Tony in everything. Why do you support him? Why do you care about him so much? Is it him or your work that you are so attached to? I see the way you two talk to each other."

"You care about him too."

"Paul you're not listening to me." She looked up into his eyes. "I love you, but I can't do this anymore."

Less than a week later, Susanna and Penny left. Paul had assumed he'd see them soon, not knowing it would be the last time he ever saw them alive. Susanna knew he chose his work over them, no matter how often he argued that he did what he did to protect them, which he truly believed. But he felt something for Tony that he couldn't synthesize.

As Paul neared home now, neared Tony, he could feel his heartbeat as the punch of the memories slowed. It felt as erratic as his breathing. He now knew why Susanna had been so willing to push the three of them apart. She knew things then that he didn't — things that Mark now had and misused violently. Perhaps, had Paul tried harder to be there for her, he would have been able to protect her from those things too.

Paul pulled into the driveway and sat staring at the damp brick of the house. His mind wandered back to the day Susanna left. Fall had been an unusually specific painting that year. It was almost as if there was a choice in where the colours had been placed in the trees that lined the streets. The city usually planted the same trees on the boulevards in front of the houses, but they seemed to change differently with the onset of cold. Some had turned a cranberry red, others golden corn. Some were the colour of pinot noir, and some were still fresh and leafy green. And then there were a few which were bare, their leaves carried by the wind and patting against the pavement, a sound which seemed to mimic the upcoming cold rain. It was as if they were trying to say, here's your last bit of colour before the dark cold of winter, brightened against a heavily saturated grey-blue sky, and remind you that you cannot always be prepared for what is to come. Sometimes, it is better not to know.

#

Paul sat at the kitchen table in Tony's seat, the morning after he had confronted Mark, two days after the bar incident. He realized he'd left Mark's birth certificate. It was 5 a.m. and Paul was waiting for Tony to wake up. He sat in the dark, allowing a final memory to flood his ears from December 23rd, 1953.

"How's Susanna?" Mark asked.

"What? She's fine, why?"

"There's some suspicion. Some staff say they've seen a woman here matching her description. They don't know where she lives yet. I'd highly suggest you keep it that way."

Paul thought his heart was about to beat up into his throat. He sped home after work and called Susanna. He hadn't spoken to her in a few months.

"Paul, hi."

"Susy, you need to leave there. You need to get as far away as possible."

"What? Slow down."

"They think you know something." There was silence on the other end. Paul continued, "You need to leave there soon."

"It's December 23rd, Paul, where would I go?"

"I don't know, just get away, please." Paul was begging now.

"Hey, everything is going to be all right." She tried to reassure him, but he could sense the worry in her voice. "We'll leave tomorrow, okay?"

"Okay."

"Thanks. I'll call you when we're somewhere safe."

"Susanna?"

"Yes?"

"I love you."

"Pen, come here." Susanna's voice distanced from the receiver and Paul could hear little feet padding across the hardwood.

"Hi, Daddy."

"Hi, beautiful. You take good care of Mommy, you understand?"

"Okay," she said. Paul heard her scurry away. He smiled, picturing her.

"Susy?" Paul almost pleaded her response.

"I love you too, Paul." She hung up the phone.

Tony's creaky bedroom door snapped Paul from his memory. Tony shuffled painfully down the hallway. Paul couldn't bear to look, waiting for him to enter the kitchen before he spoke.

"You're up early." Tony beat him to it.

"Yes," was all Paul could manage to say.

Tony turned abruptly and sat down beside him. "What's wrong?"

"I've got quite a lot to tell you," Paul's voice quivered.

Tony swallowed hard. He had things to say too. But now wasn't the time. "Tell me."

Tears fell one at a time from Paul's eyes, as he stared down at the table. Tony stood gingerly and moved his chair over to sit next to him, holding his weak arms out. Paul allowed himself to fall into them for the first time in decades. Everything spilled out about Susanna, about Mark being his brother, and about Mark knowing how to access essences. The conversation didn't intensify as Paul had expected it to. Tony just listened. They both thought of Penny and Beck. It was beautiful what existed between the four of them, and they didn't have to speak about it to know how strong it was. Their minds were simply electrical impulses, which somehow knew how to construct essences, filled with the energy of the generations before. It occurred to Tony and Paul that they hadn't sought where their own essences would go. There was something magical about the fact that essences aren't hereditary. It was no coincidence, and it would only be human to want to understand further. They hadn't worried about feeding the next generation and cultivating good memories for them. As they sat in the dark, afraid, holding one another, they knew they had been doing this all along.

"I love you, you know."

"I know."

"And?"

"I love you too, Paul." Tony was conflicted and his stomach turned. He needed to ask why Paul had been in Penny's essence, but he couldn't right now. Paul had come to him. All he could feel was Paul's hurt.

Paul was letting all these words sink in. He believed in what he had told Mark. But guilt and regret wound together, and slithered their way through his heart and weighed in his lungs.

CHAPTER 14

– Speak –

December 1979, Kingston, New Jersey

"Good morning." Tony walked into the kitchen and sat in his usual seat. He'd told Beck to stay downstairs.

"Morning," Paul answered. "You want toast?"

"No, thanks."

"You need to eat, Tony."

"I can't right now. The idea's actually nauseating."

"Well go lie down. I think Beck's gone back to sleep."

"Nope, that's not why I feel sick." Tony was stuck on the night before, but they were running out of time. He needed Paul to be truthful now.

Paul turned away from what he was doing and sat down at the table across from Tony. Tony always thought Paul's infatuation with being in the kitchen was his way of coping with life. He wondered if this was why Paul was able to be so calm in every situation.

"Please, be more articulate." Paul smiled weakly. He was concerned for Tony now. He always had been but at this point Tony's health was really a ticking time bomb. He didn't suspect that Tony had any more knowledge than he'd given him the other night.

Tony narrowed his eyes. "Is there anything else you need to tell me, doctor?"

Paul didn't turn around. "You mean, other than the fact that I have a brother who is trying to singlehandedly hoard history? And Susanna being a genius in more ways than one?"

Neither of them were prepared, but emotionally they felt the pull to talk about it now. Why, they didn't know.

"There's that. He knows how to unlock past essences, supposedly. Makes you wonder whose memories Penny has, doesn't it? Besides her own?"

Paul turned around. His voice raised slightly. "What are you playing at?"

"What's in this for you?"

"Same as you."

"No, I don't buy that."

"Excuse me?"

"You're helping him."

"Helping who?" Paul's voice was straining.

"Mark."

Paul was stunned in place.

"You feel guilty. You have no reason to. It's not your fault." Tony was on the cusp of pleading.

Paul shook his head. "You don't know what it feels like."

"You're right, I don't. But I know what the pain of guilt and regret feels like. Isn't that how we've always done this, between us? We've had different experiences, but we've felt many of the same things. Talk to me."

"We don't have time."

"When has time ever been an issue, Paul? I looked, you know? I looked. I know it's today, for both of us. And you know it too. Our lives are fleeting. It's all the more reason to set things up well for the lives after us, and now, for those who came before us."

Paul gulped. "Did you see where?"

"No, I didn't." He wasn't lying. He didn't want to know. Neither of them did and it would defeat their purpose if they did. Paul didn't respond.

Someone knocked on the door.

"Who the hell is that?" Tony sounded angry.

Paul shot Tony a look as if to say "calm down, we'll handle it." Even now, in anger, they connected together seamlessly. Paul peered out into the snow. The glass was still frosted over, so he couldn't make out who stood there, but it looked like a girl. It was mid-morning, two days after Tony and Beck had their bar incident.

"I'm opening it."

Tony nodded, gripping the wall in preparation. He knew exactly who it was. He knew this would happen eventually. The more Beck went back, the more Penny would be curious. Paul opened the door, and there she stood, dressed warmly in all black, absorbing any heat left from the moment before. Her long hair tumbled out from under her hat, and she was still frighteningly beautiful in the wise way her mother had been. There was a depth of it now that lined her face, and a few strands of silvery hair blended in with the icy exterior of the house as they swayed. The older she got, the more it became clear that she couldn't be Paul's daughter. Her black Jeep was parked in the driveway, and she stood, firmly unsurprised by who answered the door, though her eyes were damp with tears. Tony noticed that there was anger in them too.

"Hi," she said confidently, but sternly. "May I come in?" There was a sarcasm in her voice that caused both Tony and Paul to take a step back as she entered.

Paul stumbled over his words but managed to let her know that she was welcome to come in after she had already entered. Neither Paul or Tony knew what to say. They were frozen and mesmerized as if the years were coming back to them all at once.

"We need to talk," Penny said assertively, breaking the silence. She stopped and looked back and forth between them, waiting for them to say something.

"Uh, hi, Pen," Tony finally broke.

"Hi," she said, trying desperately to hide her emotions. She turned to face Paul, who had kept his distance.

"Hi, Penny," he said, cautiously reserved, even for him.

Tony shoved his hands in his pockets. "How have you been, Pen? You want something to eat or coffee or anything?"

"You've aged," she replied, searching his face for the person she'd loved so much as a child. Tony was now someone she hardly recognized. "And you can't do that."

"Do what?" Tony asked.

"Pretend like you didn't leave me. Like it hasn't been twenty-five years."

"Penny, do you think we wanted to?" There was pain in the way Tony asked her this, as if he expected her to reply cynically, but had hoped that at the very least, she'd be happy to see him.

"I don't know. How was I supposed to know? I was five," she replied coldly.

"Penny, we were trying to protect you," Paul finally added.

"Maybe you were. As in past tense." Penny glanced toward Paul who looked sheepish but also confused.

"What does that mean?" Paul shot back.

"I think you know exactly what it means."

Paul stared at her coldly but said nothing.

"In my memories there's a man, dressed in black, following me. Someone who seems to be a little more proactive than the other Sifters, someone who has a little more knowledge." Penny narrowed her gaze at Paul.

"And why would you assume that's me, Penny?"

"I didn't, until recently. You just did."

"You're quite like someone else in this room, aren't you? Same wits, same irritating sarcasm, same insecurities, and social disassociation."

Tony stared hard at Paul. He was shocked by how quickly his tone had changed. "What are you saying?"

"Oh come on, Tony. Seeing her now, you can't say you didn't know. She looks just like you."

"For one, she's much more graceful with her words than I am. That she got from you."

Penny turned toward Tony with a pained glare. "Is it true?" her voice shook. She glanced behind him to see her mother's old book of Proverbs on a shelf by the fire.

"Yes, it's true," he replied.

Paul sneered at them, his eyes filled with a dark rage that took both Penny and Tony by surprise. "You've known the whole time, haven't you?" he asked Tony. "Did you know?" He switched his gaze to Penny.

"I did." Tony looked Paul in the eyes apologetically. There was no sense denying anything now.

"I had suspicions but only when I was older," Penny answered, somewhat taken aback by the truth that was coming out in the front foyer of Tony and Paul's isolated house. She did not expect them to be living together this many years later. She actually didn't have a clue what she'd find by showing up here, aside from Beck who was nowhere in sight.

"Penny, how did you get here? How did you find us?" Tony demanded. The tension was rising.

Penny's eyes were filled with angry tears, and she struggled to speak. Tony was her father. He was the only one she wanted in her life after her mother died. He left her. And he knew.

"Me," Beck answered, emerging from the living room. He leaned against the doorway and crossed his arms.

"God, I thought I said stay downstairs!" Tony ran his hands through his hair. Paul kept his glare on both Tony and Penny. This was the first time all four of them had ever been in the same room.

"I'm sure, actually, that God has something to say about all of this," Beck answered. "One big happy family."

"I agree. Is there anything *else* you want to inform me of? You stole my parents, my daughter, and I'm just waiting around for you to die of cancer. So you're stealing yourself away from me too. Convenient."

"Well that's a bit contradictory isn't it?" Tony shot back. Paul pulled a gun from the drawer and pointed it at Penny. Tony stepped in front of her, putting his hands up. "Paul." The sarcastic temper was wrung from his voice.

Paul's arm shook and his tears fell out of an anger Tony had never seen, and one that nearly broke his heart. "I stuck by your side all this time, Tony. I loved you." Penny began to walk toward Beck who had motioned her to come to him, but Paul caught her and pointed the gun at her. "Don't you move either," he sneered through his teeth.

"And how do you feel now? Powerful? You want to kill the two people who matter most to you, Paul?" Tony demanded.

"No, I don't. But I want to make things right."

"Paul, listen to me. This won't fix anything with Mark. If you want to make this right, please help us. We can't ever fix anything. But we can set things on the right course. Please."

Paul's hand steadied on the gun and he stared blankly at Tony. An empty numbness filled his eyes.

"Biologically, yes, I'm Penny's father. But Susanna wanted you to raise her," Tony kept talking.

"Fuck you," Paul spoke more clearly than he had the whole conversation. He was no longer shaking and his eyes had dried.

"Paul. We love you. I love you so much. Please."

"You know, it doesn't matter." Paul shook the gun at Tony and took a step toward him. Tony didn't move. Paul was gritting his teeth as he spoke.

"Every moment matters."

"Her death was planned. Mark had her killed. He was trying to get rid of both of them. But I don't blame him. It's not his fault that he's like this. But with the right essences, I can help him."

"If you can forgive him, then please, forgive yourself. His experience is not your fault."

Paul turned toward Penny who backed up into the wall. She was fearfully captivated in a way Beck had never seen her. "I told your mother to get out. I told her to take you and get away and she was too late because Tony showed up." Paul's words were empty, choppy, and calm. He spoke with almost no emotion.

"She was leaving when I got there, Paul," Tony interrupted.

"You wanted the one thing I had over you. The only thing. You've taken everything from me. So I'm taking something from you. I'm taking both of them from you. And I'm going to make things right."

Paul turned the gun toward Beck who leapt behind the wall before the gunshot sounded. Tony jumped in front of Penny, holding her behind him. "You shoot me first," Tony said, knowing Paul couldn't pull the trigger. Paul pointed his gun at Tony, his hand shaking again. Looking at Tony, frail and incapable of what he was doing, Paul's eyes flickered. "I loved you!" he screamed through his teeth.

"Paul, you still do. Stop this, please," Tony pleaded, breathing irregularly. He was weakening by the minute.

"You need to pay for what you did and so do I. She's going to die anyway."

"Not yet. It's not their time. It needs to happen at the right time. You know that."

"You don't even know if it's going to mean anything!"

"You're right, I don't, but sometimes you need to trust. Please, trust me."

Paul and Tony held eye contact. He waited for Tony to fall to his knees, too weak to stand. Penny sank down to catch him.

"No, no, no," she mouthed, cradling his head. Tears rapidly filled Paul's eyes as he followed Penny's head down to the ground with the gun. Beck leapt in front of both of them, screaming in pain as his blood sprayed.

Penny gasped through her tears, almost choking as she silently watched Beck hit the floor. She still cradled her father's head in her hands.

"You little fucker!" Paul screamed. Shooting him again on the ground. Both attempts Beck had only been grazed in the leg and hip, but the scrapes in his flesh were deep. Paul aimed steadily at his head, staring at Beck writhing in pain, but he was speaking to Tony. "You put me through emotional hell."

Penny was trying to reach Beck's shoulders to pull him toward her. A gun fired and she screamed this time. "No!"

She looked down to her lap and realized Tony was no longer lying there. Her gaze darted to her left and she saw him, sitting up against the door, his eyes unrecognizably filled with pain, and his arm extended out. A gun was in his hand, pointed directly at Paul. Paul sank to the floor on his knees, dropping his gun, and bringing his hands to his chest. Penny's hands clasped over her mouth as she watched every emotion spill out of Paul's eyes as he made eye contact with Tony, and fell to the ground.

Penny crawled over to Beck who was trying to sit up.

"Hey, hey, look at me." She grabbed his face and turned it toward hers.

Beck grabbed her arms and pulled her to him. "I'm okay, I'm okay." Her body was shaking against his. She pulled away and turned to Tony, who looked deathly ill, leaning against the door.

"Are you both all right?" he asked, watching Paul take his last breaths. At the end, he turned his head away, pressing his eyes closed as hard as he could. Both Penny and Beck knew that a part of Tony had always lived for Paul.

"Are *you* all right?" Penny asked, trying to collect herself. "Where did you find that?" She motioned to the gun.

"I always had one under the tile in case something like this happened."

"Are you okay?" she repeated sternly. Tony looked into her eyes, as if to tell her he was sorry without saying it. She nodded.

"My days are numbered, but I'll manage." He sat up and leaned toward Beck.

"What do we do?" Beck mumbled, trying to sound like he wasn't in pain. "How long do we have?"

"Where are you hit?" Tony asked, ignoring his question.

"I'm fine."

"Beck, where are you hit?"

Penny looked back and forth between them, sensing a connection that she hadn't anticipated.

"My right leg. First one grazed my hip, second one hit my shin."

"Can you stand?"

"Can you?" Beck smiled at him, and Tony smiled back weakly.

"Well we're both going to need to, aren't we?"

Beck grabbed the door frame and pulled himself up, then reached down under Tony's arms and pulled him up too. He was heartbroken by how light he had become. The three of them stood for a moment, looking down at Paul. On the surface of their hearts, they mourned.

"How much time do we have, Tony?" Penny grabbed Beck's arm and wrapped it around her shoulders to help him stand.

"I'm not sure. But you need to leave here now. Penny, can you drive?" Tony sat on the small table beside the front door, gripping the door frame with the little strength he had.

"What do you mean 'you'?" both Penny and Beck asked.

"You know this is the end for me, Beck, I chose not to get treatment. I wanted this to be the last thing I did."

"But as usual you didn't think of anything anyone else wanted for you." Beck's voice wavered slightly.

"Beck, the three of us don't have much time left on this Earth. That's the demand of what we have done here. It's interesting though, come to think of it. The only difference is that we know when the end is coming, and how vital it is to know what to do with the time left. You two need to finish this. You need to stay safe for a few days more and it isn't safe here."

"We're not leaving without you," Penny said, trying to hold herself back and sound like she didn't care as much as she did, but she broke. "I just got you back."

"Pen." Tony took every ounce of his strength to stand and reach out to her. She fell into his arms.

"I'm sorry, Pen," Tony whispered, stroking her hair as he once had many years earlier. Penny felt herself forgive him, and she finally put the pieces together in her head. He really was trying to protect her and keep her safe.

"I knew you were special. I didn't know why yet, but I knew you were special. And I loved you and your mom. I want you to know that."

Penny looked up into his eyes, but she didn't need to search them for the truth. She knew he was telling it. "I know, Mr. Anthony." She smiled brightly for the first time since she last saw him, and Tony's heart crumbled at the sight of his little girl. Tony turned to Beck, who was leaning against the door, clearly in pain.

"There's peroxide and alcohol," he paused to catch his breath, "in the cabinets above the sink in the bathroom. Penny?"

"I'm on it." As she left to go find these things for Beck, Tony desperately wanted to get out everything he'd needed to say.

"Brooks? I uh…"

Beck looked up to face him. "It's okay, don't."

"No, I need to. I'll never forgive myself if I don't. You are God's gift to me. I couldn't have Penny around, but He gave me you; a piece of Susanna. But you're so much more than that. You are the son I never had." Beck didn't know what to say.

"I love you, kid. You gave me hope again. And you've given Penny hope by loving her, not saving her, and now you're going to give the world hope. Proud isn't even the right word. I'm sure Penny would have a better one."

Beck was trying not to cry, but the tears fell. He limped over and hugged Tony for the very last time. No matter how thin or weak he had become, Beck felt safe in his arms.

"And you're the father I needed," he whispered. Tony hugged him tighter, tears filling his own eyes now. They both let go once Penny returned, and Tony gave a nod to Beck, as if to say, "It's up to you now, I'm letting you go."

#

Penny treated Beck's wound as best as she could. She gave him some painkillers and wrapped his shin and hip in one of the emerald curtains from the kitchen with hot salt to stop some of the bleeding. Beck stole the idea from Penny and Susanna's scarf. The two of them carried Tony to his bed, which he was reluctant about. Beck didn't realize how much he felt at home in this house, and before he left the room he turned to ask Tony one final question, noticing his breathing had slowed considerably.

"Tony, what will happen to this house?"

"Don't worry, I've left it to a few very special people. Someone you know, I believe," he replied, and winked.

"Who?" Beck paused to think. "Mary?" he asked. Tony smiled, as he slowly lost his ability to speak. Beck sauntered in from the doorway to sit on the edge of Tony's bed. His face spelled out helplessness. Tony could hardly speak and his breathing was laboured.

"Beck, you couldn't have saved me, but you were wonderful medicine. You helped me forgive myself. Our truth is incomplete like anyone else's. But what means the most is all up here," he motioned slowly to his head, "because we paid attention with this." Tony reached over and pulled Beck's hand to his heart. "Paul and I thought we knew what we were looking for in our research. We found what Susanna and Penny could have given us all along — memories — an essence worth passing on. So much of what I gave my life to in research, always felt like it made more sense when I explained it to you." He smiled, squeezing Beck's hand, and closed his eyes. As Beck felt Tony's grip fade, he wondered why he told him this now, when Beck only had a few days to live. It occurred to him that this, too would be a memory — a powerful one that he would pass on. Who would you be to judge which are most valuable, or who needs any given one, the most?

Beck stood and walked to Penny who was now in the doorway. Beck left, but Penny paused to look at Tony, lying peacefully in the bed. She didn't have the words. She walked in slowly, taking his hands in hers, and kissing him on the forehead.

"Thank you, for putting the pen in my hands," she whispered. She wasn't sure why she felt she needed to, but she began talking to him. "You know, I've thought about all this a lot, and wondered if memories and stories would be passed on to children anyway, just by nature of them living with their parents. But I think you knew that's not always the case, for so many reasons. So many memories, experiences, and stories aren't shared, either by choice or suppression. But they are all needed. They are history." She placed Tony's hands at his sides, in his pockets, and leaned over to click on the radio beside the bed. She'd played a game with him when she was a girl, guessing the date of the song on the radio. She turned the dial, stopping on one song from 1977 as it bled into the next from 1979. She'd always wondered what Tony had thought of the transition from disco to punk, and laughed a little. She smiled at Tony one last time and headed to the foyer to join Beck.

The two of them lifted Paul's body onto the couch in the living room, and closed his eyes.

"I don't really remember much of him," Penny said. She felt for him, and all of his loss, leaning in to kiss his forehead. "I wish he wasn't in so much pain. I wish he knew how much Tony and my mom loved him."

"He was a great man," Beck added. He remembered the times Paul woke early to make him toast after a long night with Tony downstairs, and came to save them from their bar extravaganza. Beck admired how loyal Tony and Paul had been to protecting each other all these years. Both Penny and Beck realized how much they would miss the two of them, even though their time was so short. That was the thing. The strength of a relationship and your impact on someone else is never necessarily based on a long period of time, or on time at all. As Beck took Penny's hand, they both thought about how profoundly the four of them had affected one another's lives. Beck stroked the subtle grey in her hair. Their lives were connected through time in a way they'd never fully understand. Now they knew that everyone's were. Without migration, be it of people or their essences, there is no life. They needed to trust the most uncertain migration of all. A thud broke their stream of thought. Something had fallen from Paul's jacket. Penny knelt down to pick it up.

"It's my mother's." She began thumbing through the aged pages of Susanna's detailed handwriting. "It's her research." Penny hugged it to her chest. She looked down at Paul, so hurt and conflicted, but somehow still helping them.

"What are we going to do with it?" Beck asked.

"I know what to do."

"Okay. We need to keep moving."

Beck began packing some bags that he found in Paul's drawers with the last of the bread and raspberry jam. He was digging through the bags when he noticed a quilt, folded neatly in the corner of the drawer. It reminded him of something Tony had said:

"The collections of memories that we have in our minds are like my sock drawer — we have to sort through them at some point and find their pairs." The quilt was a combination of old, indecipherable clothing, and it smelled like both Tony and Paul. Beck took it with him. Penny grabbed some paper, a pen, and a plastic bag from the kitchen.

#

Fear hadn't hit them again until they were on the road in silence. Tony had mentioned to head north into populated areas, so that they could blend in. Beck almost forgot that it was present day. This wasn't a memory, but it was soon to be. They drove toward New York City in Penny's black Jeep.

CHAPTER 15

– & Give Energy –

December 1979, New York

"You know, you could have chosen a less obvious car." They had been driving in silent grief for an hour, and Beck was trying to get away from it.

"And what woman do you expect to be driving a black Jeep?"

Beck just smiled. He could hear the years in her voice as it trembled over the words. "Are you okay, Pen?"

"Define okay."

"What's on your mind?"

Penny took a deep breath. "This is happening really fast," she spoke softly, almost a whisper as she gripped the steering wheel. "I'm happy to be spending my last bit of time with someone I love, and I regret not trying to do that my whole life."

Beck smiled. "You did."

At first she didn't understand what he meant, and then realized that he had been present throughout many of her memories. She also realized that Tony had orchestrated it all. She'd been surrounded by two of the people she loved most her whole life. Beck and Tony had been shaping her the entire time — not changing her memories, but enhancing them by lifting the way she lived, the way she was curious, the way she was intentional. It dawned on her that this might be another power that essences hold, for the people they are passed to.

"You love me?" Beck added, somewhat sarcastically.

"I mean, loosely, I suppose." She smirked and they both laughed. There were a few moments of silence. "Do you know why?"

Beck just looked at her. It was an odd question. He opened his mouth to speak but then shook his head no.

Penny smiled. "Because you let me live. You listened to me. You didn't try to save me. But you were always there nonetheless."

Beck was about to speak when the dashboard beeped. They needed gas.

"How much time do we have?" Penny asked, staring out into the open road blankly. It seemed so wide and vast despite the narrowing minutes they had left.

"Thirty-two hours," Beck replied hesitantly, looking at his watch. He thought of Tony, longing to hear his voice in his ear. The mood had dampened again as the sun tumbled behind the clouds.

\#

They pulled over into a forest on the side of the road and tried to sleep overnight in the Jeep. They lay awake across the back seats and Penny nestled into Beck's side. He was trying to comfort her, feeling her fear pulsing throughout her body as they shivered from the cold. Trying to keep Penny from breaking down kept himself from doing so as well. They were both terrified, but, of course, neither would be the one to admit it. It was midnight and they had stuffed themselves with the bread and jam a few hours before. They wondered about things like eating and why they bothered if their time on this Earth was drawing to a close. They wondered why they didn't push their bodies to the limit for the sake of doing so. They both lay awake thinking the other was asleep, staring at the stars peeking through the cracks of the evergreens. They were protected by the windows of the Jeep, but no less cold. Beck stroked Penny's hair, a subtle way of saying he wanted to talk.

She whispered quietly, "I thought you were asleep."

"Back at you," he answered. "What's on your mind?"

"What's not on my mind?"

"Amen."

Penny paused and shifted her weight, resting her head on her hand, and propping both on her elbow so she could look at Beck when she talked to him. She had always made sure to do this, and more so now. Beck noticed she truly looked at you when she talked to you, which was something Tony had said Susanna always did. Beck appreciated the chance to look at the world in Penny's eyes each time.

"Have you wondered how it's going to happen?"

"How what's going to happen?" He put a piece of her hair behind her ear.

"Our deaths. How are we going to die? What if it doesn't happen when or how it needs to? Would we have to kill each other?"

"I've tried not to think about it."

"Well I think we should."

"Why can't we just let what's supposed to happen, happen?"

"Because what if we outsmart it? The assumption is we don't know about all this."

"How do you know what the universe or God assumes?"

"I don't, I suppose," she paused and looked up into the trees, "I'm just scared."

Beck hugged her tighter. "Me too," he said, "me too," and pressed his forehead and nose into hers.

"We just won't know what happens next."

"I know. But we'll have done all we can do."

Penny sat up, reaching into her bag. She pulled out her notebook and pen, along with a plastic bag.

"What are you doing?"

"Deciding what happens next." She nestled her head into Beck's shoulder and began to write. As she wrote for what seemed like an hour, Beck could feel her shaking, periodically reaching up to wipe away her tears so that they wouldn't stain the paper. When she'd finished writing, she tore the paper from her book, folded it, and placed it in the plastic bag alongside Susanna's notebook. She hugged both to her chest, as she and Beck sat in silence for a few minutes.

"Your time is right before mine, so I'll be with you until the very end. I promise." Penny nodded, nestled her head back into his arms and closed her eyes. The snow was falling and sticking to the trees. It was beautiful and peaceful. The stars and moon twinkled white light off of the untouched snow and sparkled in through the window. Beck thought about these moments. It wasn't at all about the time left ahead. It was about the time now. He knew Penny was right. *We aren't supposed to know when we are going to die.* Tony's ambition had led him to try to perfect knowledge and predictions about life out of passion and pain. He didn't see the beauty in not knowing until later. Life was worth being curious about, no matter how short and no matter how or where it was lived.

"I feel like my duty now is like draft zero of my book. I just have to exist and do my best. That's all God wants me to do," Penny spoke quietly.

"Yeah, I think you're right."

Beck leaned his head against Penny's and they started to fall asleep. He checked his watch, which showed twelve hours from 2 a.m. now. They had until 2 p.m. the next day.

"Thank you," Penny whispered.

"No, thank *you*, Pen."

As Penny fell asleep, Beck spoke softly, separating the few grey strands of her hair from the black. "You're the closest thing to magic, you know. Something wants us to learn and listen to someone trustworthy to experience and observe the world. The world will learn from you, as I have." His voice began to drift off. "They'll learn to love again, hear again, listen again, understand other's pain again, empathize again…"

#

When they woke the next morning, they started the remainder of their drive north to New York City. The tension had steeped overnight and uncertainty saturated their speech. For the most part, they were silent for the last few hours of the drive. They didn't know what exactly they were supposed to do. The only thing Tony had told them was that someone would find them and try to kill them before their time, but who would be sent to find them was unclear. Beck started thinking about how easy it would be to spot the two of them and shoot. The game would be over. They had to stay hidden until the time came. Their tension eased when they hit midday traffic on the bridge into the city and tried to blend in with the other cars. The skyline was scarcely visible from the cold moisture in the air. The temperature was a degree too cold now to snow, which created an eerie mist hovering around the city and frozen water, clearly on Penny and Beck's side, as if trying to help disguise them. They wore dark clothing and kept their hoods up. Beck was driving now because Penny was anxious. He could almost see the weight on her shoulders and how much weight had been there since she was a little girl. She sat fiddling with her prosthetic leg, tying the scarf tighter than it needed to be. She winced in pain.

"We'll find each other again. We'll find them again," Beck said, breaking the long silence. Penny nodded, looking down at her hands and flipping them over in her lap. There was so much in them. Beck looked up and nailed his breaks, reaching over and creating an arm bar across Penny's chest. The traffic had stopped, but not because there were too many cars. There were four black-windowed SUVs driving the wrong way on the freeway toward them. A man's voice echoed through the fog, bouncing between vehicles, and calling for the black Jeep to pull over. Penny and Beck looked at one another, but there was no panic in their eyes. They were looking as if to acknowledge that this would be the fight of their lives.

"This is why you don't drive a Jeep," Beck said, casually checking the rear-view mirror for how much space he had behind him. "We're going to have to get out." The SUVs were only about fifty metres ahead of them.

"They are evacuating people out of their cars, Beck."

"Perfect." Beck took a deep breath.

They both got out slowly, trying to conceal their doors by not opening them too widely for their pursuers to see. "We stay in line with the cars, and we walk toward them."

"What?" Penny was alarmed by this decision.

"People haven't been evacuated yet from their cars back here. Up there we can blend in."

"But we have to get there."

"We stay low and in line with the cars. Trust me."

Penny nodded. Beck took Penny's hand and they crouched low, below the height of the car windows and walked toward the front of the commotion. Beck thought they must have blocked the road ahead. He wondered how much these guys knew. He wondered if they knew what Penny's purpose was. Eventually, they reached the SUVs driving through the traffic, asking everyone to evacuate their vehicles. Beck gripped Penny's hand tighter and pulled her in front of him as they passed.

"What are you doing?" she whispered aggressively.

"You need to be in front."

"Why?"

"Well if they shoot they need to hit me first." With their eyes they said everything that needed to be said between them. They walked gingerly between people, not trying to weave to the front of the pack too aggressively. They heard another man's voice come onto the microphone, and everyone in the crowd paused. Based on Tony's description, it looked like Mark.

"We are looking for two fugitives. A young woman and a young man. The male is blond, and the woman has black hair and a prosthetic leg. They are together, on the run, and dangerous."

The crowd started mumbling and looking around, everyone ready to throw the other into the hands of the authority. Beck gripped Penny's hand so tightly she almost pulled it away, but she let him guide her through the crowd. They kept their hoods up despite their vague descriptions. They were getting close to the front and Beck began to panic. He could see the bridge blocked off with barricades. Whoever was there wasn't about to just let them escape through. He slowed his walk to almost a stop as his eyes darted around for a way out. He looked down at his watch. They only had a minute left. Of course, whoever was after them knew this too and Penny grabbed Beck's arm tightly, turning him around to see men in black suits and bulletproof jackets aggressively cutting the crowd and running toward them. Beck turned to see the same from their end. The people seemed to part the Red Sea around Penny and Beck. Beck grabbed Penny and turned her around to face him. He clasped his hands around her jaw and kissed her forehead.

"I love you." Tears tumbled freely down their faces as fear gripped their throats. They were afraid they wouldn't know if they were successful.

"The bridge," Beck said, strangely calm, still holding her face in a sea of strangers who now stared in awe at what was unfolding around them. Penny nodded, her eyes pressed together now. Beck scooped her into his arms to shield her with his body and ran toward the edge of the bridge. They felt as if they were moving in slow motion, hearing the dulled sound of guns firing toward them at will, ricocheting off of the concrete, parked cars, and lodging themselves into Beck's back and shoulders. Penny screamed as Beck bled, as if she felt his pain. But he still ran, swinging the two of them over the side of the bridge. Penny held onto his waist, as Beck held onto the edge of the bridge. As pain seared through his body, and as the blood drained from him, he caught a glimpse of the last few seconds ticking on the watch. Penny slipped from his grip and he caught her with the other arm that had been hit and screamed in pain. He looked down into her eyes, and she glanced back, tears flowing. She looked at him calmly.

"It's okay." Penny smiled with the brightness she'd had as a girl. Beck never let go of her gaze as he used every last ounce of his strength and life to let her fall, watching her body smash through the glassy ice as gracefully as one could. Moments later, once his clock ran out, he let go too.

#

Their bodies washed up on shore a few hours later, next to a man ice-fishing near his cottage. As he searched them for identification on the shore, he found something in Penny's jacket. He pulled out a small plastic bag with a piece of paper and a red leather notebook inside. The man sat in the frozen sand reading it, tears falling down his cold cheeks. He nodded at Penny, hoping that in some way she could hear him. He folded the paper back up and placed it back in the plastic bag. He tucked it securely into her jacket and the notebook into his. He lifted both Penny and Beck into a sled and walked out to the deepest part of the water he could get to. He placed Penny's hand in Beck's, and tied them together with rope. He broke a perfect circle in the ice, and with a few spare pieces of rock, placed them back in the water. As their bodies sank, the man noticed a necklace lifting away from Beck's neck, glittering against the ivory-black water. It was a pen pendant. He remembered the name signed on the letter: Penny. He sat on the ice, and though he had never been a religious man, he prayed.

#

Fourteen years later, in the spring of 1993, a small package of documents arrived at three thousand front doors across the world, for three thousand fourteen-year-old kids. The first sheet of paper read:

You've likely heard a version of the story of Anthony and Penny Crypt, Paul Elliott, and Becker Brooks. It's a story that's difficult to explain. Please read the following clipping from December of 1979.

FUGITIVE NASA SCIENTISTS ANTHONY CRYPT AND PAUL ELLIOT FOUND DEAD.

Dr. Anthony Crypt and his research partner, Dr. Paul Elliott, part of the Sifting Project, were found dead in their home Thursday morning. Crypt's daughter, Penny, and his mentee, Becker Brooks, are presumed dead after leaping over the Brooklyn Bridge yesterday afternoon. Their bodies have not been found. The Sifting Project, an unprecedented, dangerous, and unauthorized initiative is under investigation. The U.S. Department of Defence assures that there is no cause for concern. This project was conducted without authorization and will be terminated.

This story became famous the year you were born, as did the books you now read in school about essences being beautiful hereditary trajectories. This is not the truth. Essences cannot be hereditary, which is part of their beauty. The Sifting Project still operates and is used in response to a fear of war, to gain worldwide intelligence, and to silence the mistakes of the past. Essences of the past, within you, can be unlocked now at the hands of those with power, giving them more agency over truth than they've ever had. The process harms millions of people in the process without them knowing, as natural essence trajectories are manipulated. Dr. Crypt had hoped he could change this, and he did. These are Penny's words, written the day before she died and preserved until now, for you:

To you, when you're ready,

I am writing this in my jeep in December of 1979, the night before I will die. You're wondering how I could possibly know this and I have to be honest, it is still a bit unclear to me. But it feels right. And so I trust it. I've always been a poet, and a rather lonely one, ridden with trauma and heartbreak — this is the same old story. There are also beautiful, intricate threads of joy in my heart. The commonality here is that these are all memories, which come together to compose the essence of who I am. This may sound whimsical, but imagine: What if this biologically happened within each of us? What if our stories survived, accumulating more memories and more depth, taking their final form as biological essences somewhere inside of our minds when our time on this Earth dwindles? What if we could pass this essence on when we die? In a very odd, convoluted way, I have learned that we can. Bear with me.

There was a time, I think, when people were drawn to the stories that held the truth passionately, in the hands that passed it through generations. They were motivated by a fear of forgetting. We believed in the food of our ancestors, teaching us to give our own. We believed in gardening for everyone who would come after us in our lineage. Human memory is a long, complex story, biologically flowing through each of us, carrying the ripples and waves of those who came before. Until now, we thought these memories were merely passed through generations by word of mouth, writing, and art. It so happens that they are physically stored inside of us. We've known, since 1942, that the environments, hardships, pain, loss, and starvation of a given generation are carried through the bodies of our kin via epigenetics. But there is more. As we carry our direct ancestor's physical trauma in our own bodies, so we carry the stories and memories of the past in our minds. Epigenetic changes flow from mother and father to child. Essences, comprised of the essence of who we are: stories and memories, flow from person to person at a random we cannot hope to understand — there is beauty in not being able to predict these trajectories. However, many have tried to manipulate them and change them preferentially due to fear, uncertainty, and the search for power and control. A scientific discovery, by my father, unsurprisingly went awry when grasped in the wrong hands. This has made us fearful that many stories are lost to time, oppression, and tampering. But many have survived within us, waiting to be unlocked. This is what I, my father, his best friend, and my soulmate fought to protect. You must carry the torch now, keeping the flame. Be wary of who the wind, which might blow out the flame, is coming from.

This is a beauty we must carry wisely, delicately, and compassionately. We do not know whose essences we have inherited, filled with truth and experiences we likely do not know, or ones which contradict what we thought we did. We must carry and acknowledge the truth in the past and simultaneously allow it to teach us what it is meant to, or exist in the way it was meant to. All the while we must cultivate the best memories and stories we can, for who we will give them to next. Do not take for granted your chance to wonder at the world. Seek all of its joys and understand joy's complicated roots. Look for joy and preserve and protect the stories of it inside of you, because it is power against those who seek to take it.

Perhaps it is now time to listen, as something seems to be trying to correct us, feeding memories to someone who needs it, and to the one who can do something with it. Essences give us the chance to see what it is like to view the world through eyes which are not our own. Look from another side to hear, feel, and see them.

My essence followed an unusual trajectory — it didn't approach just one person. Tomorrow, it will spread across the world. I don't quite understand why. Perhaps the reason is more strongly rooted in the essences I carry along with my own. All I know, is that my essence will flow through you. So many people's truths are inside of you — we could never know which ones until now. Now, we know many of them are stories and memories which have been silenced. And so, this is the task I leave to you. Separate who you are, from what is inside you, growing like a plentiful beanstalk to lift you higher, so that you may do the same for it. From high up, you can see the fractured picture and records of the past which we are taught. You can also see the truth, including your own — books unwritten until given the chance.

My father, as he researched and discovered many of these things, taught me to hold passion in my hands while in pain and to fight for what is right, even if the direction is unclear. His best friend taught me that good people make difficult choices and are led to dangerous places because they are afraid — this doesn't make them bad people. My soulmate taught me to love people and lift them up for who they are, unconditionally and without expectation — he taught me that I could be a hero just by being. My mother taught each of us, that gaining the same power as those who have it, does not make us equal. Perhaps this is why I was chosen. I don't know whose memories flow through me, but I do know that there is magic in them alongside my own, in the way they may influence you and enable you to lead.

This is my letter to you: the world, which hasn't written back to me, among many other people. You may choose not to trust me — a poet with no scientific background of my own to prove my words. But we must know by now that science imitates art, as art imitates science. Throughout this whole story, science seems the flaw, but it isn't. The pursuit of it is, when unwilling to trust anything else. Essences are beautiful, you know. We never had to speak about them or research them to somehow feel that they existed. I never had to unlock the ones within me to feel them. Perhaps this is the perfect ending: science and poetry coming together to unlock the essences in you. People will believe in a story if the hero is tangible. I didn't want to be a hero. But I've seen that I didn't have to do anything outside of myself to be one. We must believe that there are essences of others inside of us, because there are. They are heroes for fighting for their story for so long. You have the means, now, to be curious enough to lift them. You have the means, now, to reverse the virality of adulterated history. Stay on that path. I will always be there with you.

Until we meet again, in memory,

- Penny

This is your invitation. We invite you to Sift, a school where you will learn to unlock the essences inside you for good. Bundles of stories and memory ought to flow throughout the world, between and from everyone. Memories are carried from person to person and have been for thousands of years. They need only be activated. They ought to seek to destroy the ignorance-ridden communities of power and dominance. They ought to give power. We cannot be afraid of a coat that is too big for us, or a plan which we do not understand. There is hope. And it is in your hands. Carry it well.

THE END

What could Sift look like for you?